SENTINEL EVENT

a paranormal thriller

Samantha Shelby

Heather –
Witness The
Event
Samantha Shelby

THEY WON'T

STOP

CHAPTER 1

Dr. St. Cross, the psychiatrist, would have found it ironic that Tammy was watching the news report on the TV in the waiting room when the ambulance arrived. Chester Williams, a leading expert in Passerism, had given a speech at the anti-Passer protest in Denver earlier that morning, and choice segments were being replayed throughout the evening.

"No one can argue," he was saying with educated eloquence in a long-suffering tone, "that our lives have become more meaningful and safer with the help of the spirits, to whom we owe so much and can offer so little. Our world has made progress in leaps and bounds since the first of the Passers began visiting and speaking to us. It saddens me that so many of you believe otherwise."

The image lingered on Williams while the sound of the news anchor's reportage continued; Chester's eyes showed keen irritation. He pursed his lips and sighed deeply just before the scene cut away.

Tammy had come looking for a patient's son in this waiting room, and hadn't found him, but had paused to sit down on a chair and retie her tennis shoe while listening to the news report. When the sound of the ambulance's sirens reached her ears, the nurse broke away from the distraction and ran out into the receiving hall to help.

Two paramedics, both young and newly minted, pushed in through the doors rolling a patient on a stretcher.

"Twenty-nine-year-old male," one of the EMTs told the ER doctor who came to oversee. "Attempted suicide by hanging. Found by a neighbor in the nick of time, who initiated CPR."

Tammy moved closer to get a look at the face behind the bag attached to the intubation tube in his mouth.

"I know him," the doctor said before the nurse had a chance to. "He's in here all the time."

"Never self-inflicted injuries, though," agreed Tammy. The stretcher was swiftly wheeled into one of the critical care rooms. "Are you sure it was suicide?"

Without speaking, one of the paramedics lifted the patient's right arm by the wrist. Taped to the back of his hand was a piece of note card on which was clearly printed, *They won't stop.*

"'They?'" asked the other EMT.

"The Passers," answered Tammy.

"He *claims* it's the Passers," the doctor talked over her. "This is private information that we're not allowed to discuss. Patient confidentiality."

The paramedics scrunched their foreheads and shrugged, but left the doctor and nurses to do their work. While the former checked the patient's chest with his stethoscope and another nurse bagged the patient, Tammy paused to stroke the young man's brown hair off his forehead.

"Poor Aidriel," she murmured.

Outside the open door, the ghostly figure of a Passer peered out from behind a curtain at the end of the corridor. It turned and walked away, vanishing through a wall.

The days passed with Aidriel alive and alone, spending hours staring off into space. Doctors and the other patients alike showed little interest in him, and eventually, how many days later, he didn't know, he found himself in a familiar ward, on the 4th floor among the crazies. He didn't spend any time in the main room with the couches where the visitors were. No one came to see him, and he was ashamed of the bruises on his neck and jaw; the evidence of his failure.

Aidriel resented the fact he was alive. He had only survived as long as he had because of happy accidental discoveries or miraculous rescues. When he was unconscious, the air gone from his lungs, the pulse gone from his heart, and the life fading from his brain, the Passers would save him. Indirectly, that is. They would alert anyone nearby and he'd be brought back at the last moment. Eventually, he began to think of those visits past the threshold of death as if they were dreams. Dreams of strange visions and of what awaited him when he escaped life. If only he *could* escape.

He was sitting cross-legged on his bed, staring out the window, when the patient named Clifford first came to see him. The mad, bearded old man peeked around the doorframe, mumbled something unintelligible, and widened his eyes maniacally when he saw Aidriel.

Aidriel turned to acknowledge the uninvited visitor, his face blank, his gray eyes pained.

Glancing up and down the hall to make sure no one was watching, Clifford slipped silently into the room and moved to stand right behind Aidriel. The old man looked closely at the younger, saw the marks on his neck and the edge of a previous scar barely visible beneath his collar.

"It's you, finally," Clifford said. "I knew this would happen."

"What are you talking about?" Aidriel whispered, his voice still hoarse from his ordeal.

"*Them*," answered Clifford. "You know what I'm talking about. There haven't been any of them in this ward since you got here."

"Leave me alone," murmured Aidriel. "You old fart."

Clifford reached out to lay his hand on the other patient's shoulder, and Aidriel flinched. Clifford smiled knowingly and left.

Later that evening, Tammy came up to visit Aidriel when her shift ended. He showed little sign of pleasure to see her, and turned his eyes once more to the window. The kindly nurse had been on duty most of the occasions he was brought to this hospital, and knew his history. She'd also been around long enough to remember his first time, when he was seventeen. He was a happier person then.

"How are you?" she asked, lingering in the doorway.

"Fine" was his whispered reply. He didn't want to talk to her. Tammy was just like the rest of

8

the hospital staff; she pretended to believe him if she thought it would be of comfort. But he wasn't naïve enough to think she actually *did* believe him.

Once, she had seemed willing to believe, though. Aidriel was in the emergency room with a broken tibia, blunt force trauma, and she was helping prepare his leg to be set. She noticed the claw-mark scar on his forehead, and realized it had never been there before.

"What happened to your face?" she'd asked, reaching impulsively toward him. Aidriel had caught her hand defensively, and though he said nothing, he had recalled the cause of the wound.

One of Aidriel's many professions over the years was maintenance in one of the old government buildings downtown. The crawl space beneath the structure was long and narrow, and the plumbing and wiring pipes ran along the top of it. There had been problems with intermittent telephone failures, and Aidriel and two other maintenance workers had gone down to investigate.

Aidriel had been elected to get into the crawl space, mostly because he was the smallest and least lazy of the three. He'd put on a hard hat and headlamp, securing his gloves and tool belt. While the other two men lingered, shooting the breeze, Aidriel had climbed into the narrow tunnel and begun his inspection of the communication cables.

For several minutes he'd crawled along with little thought of his surroundings. He could faintly hear his colleagues talking over the sound of his own breathing, but when he stopped breathing to wet his lips, he heard another voice. Straining to see down the tunnel, he thought he could detect movement outside the range of his lamp. A familiar

9

sick feeling overtook him and he heard ringing in his ears. Though he had begun to frantically back up, he wasn't fast enough. From out of the darkness ahead rushed a Passer, pale and translucent, like all the spirits, galloping on its hands and knees like an animal. It resembled an old woman with empty white eyes, its mouth open in a blood-curdling shriek, its ghostly fingers reaching out to claw him.

The other two workers heard Aidriel screaming, and, peering into the crawl space, they saw him lying several yards into it, panicking and trying to back up.

"What's going on?" they shouted.

"Pull me out!" Aidriel yelped back.

After a brief, bewildered hesitation, the nearest worker dove into the crawl space, grabbing Aidriel by the leg and dragging him out to safety. Aidriel collapsed to the floor, shaking and breathless. His face and arms were streaked in blood and scratches; his headlamp was broken. He was too disturbed to explain what happened besides saying, "Passer."

His coworkers didn't believe him.

"Did you try to kill yourself?" the police officer asked Aidriel when he regained consciousness after the hanging. He was still in the medical wing, and they'd removed the ventilator. It hurt to breathe or swallow or talk, but he nodded.

"Why?" Tammy asked him. The policeman directed an icy stare at her, and she turned her attention back to the IV bag she was changing. She didn't notice the expression of pain and betrayal on Aidriel's face.

"You know why," he whispered to her. Tammy's attempt at compassion came off as condescending.

"The Passers don't want to hurt anyone," she told him. "They're here to help and guide us so that they can pass on into eternity."

Aidriel couldn't argue with her and simply shook his head. He'd harbored a childish resentment for her since and didn't care when she came to see him. She had come into the room and sat beside him the first time, but because of the cold shoulder she'd gotten in return, she now remained standing in the doorway.

"Most Passers stay away from hospitals," she said, as she often had before.

"Most," he muttered bitterly.

"The old assumptions of hauntings, being bound to a certain location, are false, you know."

She'd said that before as well. Many times. Everyone knew that anyway. Children learned about Passers the same way they'd learn about their own families, because so often the spirits lived like members of the households they watched over.

Even though these ghostly companions only existed in cases of violent deaths, many Passers eventually avoided the locations of their actual passing away. Often they lingered in sites of meaning, particularly old houses or cemeteries, until they answered an unspoken call to their living companion. Sometimes their death was of little meaning to them, and they were not of much comfort to the sick or mourning. It was a strange concept that had often been discussed in detail among scholars, but no cut-and-dried explanation had ever been ascertained.

11

"Is it at all reassuring to you that Matilda sends good wishes?" asked Tammy, referring to her own Passer. Aidriel had fortunately never seen Matilda as far as he knew, nor did he care to.

Rising off the bed, Aidriel moved to the door and slowly closed it, shutting Tammy out. Waiting near it for a moment and hearing nothing from her, he wandered over to the window and peered down into the parking lot. Visitors and medical workers came and went here and there, though there were no Passers that he could see. As he watched the darkness gathering, he became aware of one visible ghost. It stood unmoving in the shadow beneath a tree beside the parking lot, staring toward the building. Aidriel knew it was looking right at him; he shuddered and the hair on his arms stood up.

Eventually the spirits would grow impatient; they always did. He could only stay safe in the hospital for a certain amount of time before the Passers would break their own boundaries and come looking for him.

Clifford sat down on the bed the second time he came to see Aidriel, and received a glance of indifference for his trouble. The old man held out his arms, the insides of which were crisscrossed with scars and recent wounds.

"These," he said, pointing at the fresh scabs, "are because of you."

Aidriel looked from Clifford's arms to his face, but pretended to be unmoved. Clifford smiled wide, exposing large yellow teeth behind his tangled beard.

"It's alright," he murmured, his voice trembling with emotion. "I'm glad to finally meet you. It's been a long time coming. A long, long time."

Aidriel turned away and closed his eyes. Getting up to leave, Clifford warned him, "You have only hours left. They are slow sometimes, but they always arrive."

CHAPTER 2

Night fell and wore on slowly into the wee hours. Aidriel slept shallowly and awoke agitated, rising to pace around his room. He hated the quiet and the shadows. He measured the time not by the hours but by how long his recovery was taking, and how often he was visited. He was in no hurry to leave, but soon it wouldn't matter where he was.

At a soft knock on the doorframe he looked up to see a brunette in scrubs carrying a little organizer tote.

"Hi, I'm Dreamer from the lab," she said. "I'm here to draw some blood."

She paused as if waiting for his reaction, and he wondered if she expected a comment about her name. He understood how being constantly asked about one's moniker could quickly grow tiresome. There was no point in making small talk. Besides, it still hurt to speak.

Aidriel passively sank down onto his bed, keeping his eyes on her. She approached with a hint of shyness, and he noticed as she put on her gloves that her hands were shaking.

"Could you spell your last name for me, please?" Dreamer asked softly. She set her supply tray on the chair beside his nightstand and began preparing the items she'd need without looking at him.

"A-K-I-M-O-S," he whispered. She looked up questioningly, but saw the marks on his throat and just nodded and smiled, thanking him.

Dreamer's hands steadied as she positioned his arm on the bedside table, tying on a tourniquet, softly speaking—or rambling, he thought—about what she was doing.

"You've got great veins," she murmured with a smile.

Aidriel wasn't listening to her, and had turned so he could better hear the hallway, his eyes to the side and fixed on the door. The ward was very still, and over the classical music drifting from far away somewhere, his ears caught the whisper of ragged breathing.

Instantly, Aidriel became restless and flinched away from Dreamer, who paused patiently and apologized. With a calm warning, she inserted a needle into his vein and attached a tube, waiting for the stream of blood to fill it.

"Do you work with animals?"

She was trying to make conversation, noticing the claw marks on his skin. Aidriel was mostly ignoring her, but perceived the pause in her words while she waited for an answer. He shook his head and whispered, "Hurry up."

He was still watching the doorway when the Passer came to stand in it. The spirit was a middle-aged man with long hair and long nails. He was wheezing loudly and had a glower of hatred on his face. Everyone had a Passer; this was Aidriel's.

Dreamer glanced up at him uncomfortably and noticed his anxiety. She followed his gaze to the door, but saw nothing there.

16

"Is it a Passer?" she asked, removing the tube from the needle to push on another. "Bothering you, is it? They don't cause these, do they?" She indicated his injuries.

Aidriel was startled that she knew immediately what was wrong, and was turning to say so when the Passer attacked.

The spirit came flying forward in a blur, a guttural growl rising in its throat. Aidriel jerked swiftly to try and get away, but found himself cornered by Dreamer and the nightstand. His sudden movement pulled the needle in the phlebotomist's hand out of his arm, but he didn't notice the blood streaming out of the puncture wound.

There was no protection against a Passer attack, though it was human nature to at least attempt self-defense. Aidriel was not unused to being treated harshly, but had endeavored unsuccessfully to fight back before. There could be no trading of blows with the spirits. The result was always frustration or despair and inevitable harm.

The ghost leapt up onto the bed and clawed at him, snarling and howling, swiping its hands up and down like a slashing cat. Aidriel pulled his legs up against his chest and wrapped his arms around his head, shouting for the Passer to stop. Sometimes it heeded him; more often it didn't.

Dreamer had shrunk back in shock at the spectacle, and Aidriel accidentally kicked her in his initial attempt to protect himself. The needle in her hand flew up toward her face but fortunately didn't poke her. She had the presence of mind to snap the safety cover over the sharp end and discard it.

"What's happening?" she asked, stepping back to avoid Aidriel's defensive swings. He didn't answer her, and she saw that the tourniquet was still tied around his arm, causing profuse bleeding and purpling in his fingers. Without thinking, Dreamer reached out for the rubber strip, and her hand passed through the invisible shoulder of the Passer. Enraged, the ghost turned on her and slashed several times at her arm before Aidriel realized the Passer was actually harming her, and intervened.

His first attempt to block the blows with his own arms proved futile. Seeing no other option, Aidriel scrambled forward, shoving Dreamer as hard as he could out of the way. The young woman had managed to catch the end of the tourniquet, and being thrown off balance helped her to pull it loose, but it tangled in Aidriel's sleeve. He reached for the night table to prevent his fall off the bed and onto the phlebotomist heaped on the floor.

The Passer took a few more swings at the side of Aidriel's face before two orderlies came running into the room in response to the ruckus. At the sight of the patient balanced precariously over the phleb on the floor, they reached across the bed and seized Aidriel by his other arm. The Passer was between the hospital workers and its target, but it turned invisible when two more physical bodies came in contact with it. The attack ended.

Aidriel and Dreamer were scratched and bloodied, both shaking and incapable of answering any of the orderlies' or responding nurse's questions. Aidriel was vaguely aware of the restraints they placed on him to keep him bound to the bed. A droopy-lipped nurse told him that it might be temporary as she bandaged the deep gouges in his skin. Dreamer had already been led away, and while Aidriel listened and watched the door for a return he wouldn't see, he was uncomplaining.

Though he loathed admitting it, he was relieved. No one had ever been directly influenced by his Passer like that before. Often well-meaning people had tried to restrain or even protect him, but none of them had caused any change in the Passer, neither had they been affected themselves. But Dreamer felt the claws too. Now someone would believe him.

A woman in a lab coat sat down noisily beside Aidriel's bed while he was drifting off to sleep and abruptly awakened him. Her hair was styled in an elaborate twisting updo secured with bobby pins, and a pair of tortoiseshell glasses was balanced on the end of her nose. She reviewed her clipboard in silence for several minutes while he looked around dazedly.

"Would you prefer to be called Aidriel or Mr. Alkimos?" she asked in a no-nonsense tone.

Aidriel just shrugged and ran his tongue over his lips. They must have given him some kind of sedative and it was making him groggy.

"Mr. Alkimos it is, then."

"*Ak*imos," he corrected her.

"Ah. Right." She wrote a few quick notes, then crossed her legs at the knee. "I'm Dr. Ana deTarlo. I'm a psychologist, and will be taking over your mental health treatment for the time being."

"Dr. St. Cross is my shrink," he murmured.

"St. Cross has retired and has yet to be permanently replaced."

"He was here a few weeks ago."

"There was an accident," Dr. deTarlo said, looking distracted. "Why did you attack the phlebotomist?"

"I didn't." Aidriel's voice was improving.

"You didn't." It was obvious by the psychologist's manner that she didn't believe him.

"My Passer did."

"Your *Passer* attacked the phlebotomist."

Her tone was making Aidriel angry, and it didn't help that he was still bound to the bed and wanted to sleep.

"Yes, my *Passer* did it. It attacks me all the time; all Passers do. But all of you quacks and eggheads brush it off and tell me I'm wrong. I'm *not* wrong, you're all just too damn arrogant to listen to me."

"What's your Passer's name? Is it nearby, that I might have a talk with it?"

She pretended to look around the room in case the ghost was visible to her. Aidriel didn't answer for a long time and glared at the shrink.

"Its name is Rubin," he spat finally. "If it was around, it'd be sharpening its claws on me."

Dr. deTarlo didn't seem to be listening, and was writing on her clipboard.

"Have you been vigilant in taking your antidepressants?"

"No."

"Why is that?"

"Because I'm not depressed."

The faintest of smiles curled one side of deTarlo's lip as she transcribed.

"Why did you attempt to take your own life, then?"

Aidriel shifted uncomfortably and looked listless.

"Your wording makes it sound like I tried to steal something," he evaded.

"Suicide is illegal."

"That only encourages people to make sure they're successful."

"Is that why you tried to hang yourself? To break the law?"

Aidriel began to laugh, his voice rough. It hurt to use his throat that way, but he was too bitterly affected to stop at first.

"That is the dumbest theory for suicide I've ever heard," he commented. Ana allowed the slightest hint of agitation to show on her face.

"Why did you try to kill yourself?" she asked again, her tone relaxing.

"I know you'll be shocked by the answer," replied Aidriel with hostile sarcasm, "but I tried to kill myself because I want to be *dead*."

DeTarlo effortlessly smoothed any expression off her face.

"And why do you want to be dead?"

"You've got my file. Do your research."

"You claim that the Passers attack you."

"Yeah, I *just* told you that."

"Passers are not aggressive like ghosts used to be."

"You and I are not talking about the same Passers."

"Know Passers well, do you?"

Aidriel chuckled humorlessly.

"You could say that."

"Do you want to die to become a Passer?"

Aidriel stared at her in unpleasant surprise before answering. It never failed to shock him when a shrink said something to him that was more out-there and crazy than anything he could fathom. Perhaps psychosis was contagious.

"I want to die," he said, lowering his voice, "because life's a burden, and death is better."

"How can you know?"

"I've done it before. It can be sudden or gradual, but peace overtakes the fear and pain. It's like a dream that is all the more intoxicating and vivid because it's real."

"Have you been planning your suicide for some time?"

She had not heard a word he had said. He wondered what she *would* hear.

"For years," he answered indifferently.

"Why haven't you tried before now?"

Aidriel allowed the emotional reaction to the question to sink in without realizing it, and once more showed a glimpse of vulnerability.

"I never thought I'd need to," he murmured painfully. "I have lived for years believing I would be dead by the next day. If I only have today, there's not much point in killing myself."

That seemed to be a satisfactory response for deTarlo, who persisted in her detailed note-taking. The longer she wrote in uncaring silence, the more the tenderness of Aidriel's emotional wound turned to the heat of anger. She wasn't taking him at all seriously.

"I'll be reviewing your psychiatric record and talking to you further about these 'attacks,'" she informed him finally.

22

"How lucky for me," he bitingly answered.

Without replying, deTarlo got to her feet and left, passing Clifford loitering outside the door as she went. She noticed how paranoid the old man looked, but it was not an unfamiliar sight to her. Halfheartedly she shooed him away, though he came right back once she was out of sight.

Making sure no one else was nearby, Clifford stepped into Aidriel's room and swung the door closed behind him. Aidriel pulled against his binds, watching his visitor distrustfully.

"Now don't resist this, I've been waiting for this for a long, long time," Clifford stammered, looking around tensely. His arms had new scratches on them, and his face was injured also. He fumbled in the waistband of his pants, and brought out a pair of desk scissors.

Aidriel took in a deep shaky breath, but didn't speak. He kept his eyes locked with Clifford's, hoping the old man would snap out of whatever psychotic state he seemed to be in. He recognized that look; he'd almost succumbed to it himself. But being in that state of mind for the brief time when he had indulged in it was far scarier than being aware and sober. There weren't any rules in that no-man's-land of insanity; no hope or lies to lessen the anxiety. The paranoia of what *could* happen had almost become worse than what actually did.

Clifford held the scissors carefully in his knobby hand and examined them, exposing his yellow teeth in a smile again. It was anyone's guess how he had managed to obtain a pair of such dangerous implements and why he wasn't in a straitjacket in solitary. He drew nearer to Aidriel, who tightened up in an effort to lean away.

"I want to tell you something first," Clifford said, sitting on the edge of the bed, still scrutinizing the blades. Aidriel scowled and opened his lips defensively, but remained quiet. He had, with difficulty, overcome this sort of mental torment, and he did not at all wish to fall victim to it again simply because this old guy had failed to resist it as he had.

"There were many of us at the beginning," began Clifford, "and we've been dwindling down, passing our portion of the burden on to the next one and making their load heavier."

He adjusted his grip on the handle of the scissors as if preparing to do something.

Aidriel didn't want it to be this way. He had spent hours planning his suicide, and stabbing had not been high on his list of ways to do it. Besides, if he was going to be stabbed at all, he wanted to be sure he would actually die of it. Judging by the half-brained manner of Clifford's actions, Aidriel was not willing to trust the blow would be fatal and not just exceedingly painful.

"Hey!" he called out, trying to sit up. "Could someone get in here?"

Groping with his bound hand for the remote with the call button for the nurses caused the heavy wand to slip out of his reach and fall off the edge of the mattress. The straps around his wrists were too tight to allow him to press the button on the side of the bed.

"Don't you understand what I'm saying?" Clifford asked. "I mean there were others of us. Others tormented and ignored, written off as crazy, delusional."

"You don't seem to be in your right mind to me," Aidriel answered.

Clifford just smiled again and sighed heavily, looking wistfully around the room.

"I've had enough of it," he said. "Your arrival's my chance for escape."

"Someone get in here!" Aidriel yelled out again, ignoring the pain it caused to his voice.

Clifford turned the scissors in his hand so his fingers were wrapped around the handles while the blades pointed down. He raised his arm, his eyes on Aidriel's face, and murmured, "There used to be two of us."

He swung with surprising force for an old man, jamming the scissors without a hint of hesitation into his own stomach.

"Someone *get in here*!" Aidriel yelled again, straining against the straps on his arms and legs. He couldn't break his gaze away from Clifford's eyes and watched as the life drained out of the old man's face like a tap being shut off. Clifford clung to the edge of the bed for several painful minutes, his focused attention on Aidriel, who was helpless to do anything but attempt comfort.

"It gets better," Aidriel tried to ease the old man's obvious fears. "It can be better on the other side."

Clifford grunted a couple times in response before too much of him was gone and the heat went out of him. His weak form crumpled to the floor with a low wheeze.

Though Aidriel began once more to shout for help, it seemed that an eternity was passing and no one was coming. He couldn't see Clifford's face when the other man fell to the floor, but saw the

25

ghostly mist forming around the body. Death was transforming the person swiftly into a Passer, and already Aidriel could see the pale silhouette rising back to its feet.

"Someone help!" he yelled. This was not at all how he wished for things to be, and though he envied Clifford's flawless execution, he knew it could not be the same for him. Passers were not like humans, that way. The wounds they inflicted were different.

Clifford's Passer was at first confused to find itself upright once again, but realizing what state it had changed to, its expression took on a glower of hatred. It happened even to the nice Passers. Technically, all Passers were nice, when they weren't in close proximity to Aidriel. Even Clifford, a man himself tormented by the spirits while he was alive, became vicious and violent now that he was dead.

"It passes on," the spirit told him. It looked down at its hands and saw the nails were long, like all the other angry Passers. It held a paranormal equivalent of the bloody scissors still in its hand, and glanced from them up to Aidriel. The hatred deepened.

Aidriel dropped back to the bed and closed his eyes, bracing himself for what he knew would happen next. He felt the bed shake when the Passer leapt up on top of him, pressing down so firmly it was hard to breathe. The first stab to his chest surprised him and he opened his eyes, staring up at Clifford.

"There were two of us," the ghost stated angrily, stabbing again and again with the transparent weapon. "I pass my burden to you."

Each blow felt as real as any natural blade would. Aidriel couldn't breathe or call for help, and the metallic flood of blood in his mouth was spilling out at the corners of his lips. He turned his head to the side, unable to close his eyes but unwilling to look at the Passer anymore. It caught his notice that the battery-operated clock on the bedside table had stopped, and as the attack continued, the tube lightbulb in the wall fixture above his bed shattered.

The door to the room finally opened; a nurse and two orderlies appeared, stopping to stare in shock at Clifford's body on the floor and the effect the Passer was having on Aidriel. With a shriek, the nurse fled.

"Oh my god," one of the orderlies murmured, dropping to his knees beside Clifford and checking for a pulse.

"We need help in here, stat!" shouted the other, gripping Aidriel's shoulders and trying to hold him still.

"Is he seizing?" the first asked.

"Must have bit his tongue," the second answered. "Look at all that blood."

Aidriel wanted to tell them that they were wrong; it was his lungs. He couldn't breathe.

The Passer stabbed him with the scissors twice more after the arrival of the orderlies, then stopped in its attack and leaned in closely.

"All the burden," it whispered in an inhuman voice, "is yours."

Aidriel felt as if his chest was deflating like a punctured life raft. His eyes remained focused on the clock on the table. The Passer stepped back to watch, still frothing with hate.

The movement in the room continued on around the patient and his tormentor. He remained conscious, but very little registered. He'd stopped breathing, and when a defibrillator was brought in, it failed, just like the clock had. Though he could not see the Passer, Aidriel could hear its hissed wheezing. It faded away as the room became more vibrant. Once the Passer was gone, Aidriel could breathe again.

"That," panted a nurse, holding Aidriel's wrist and shaking, "was the scariest thing I've ever witnessed."

That night in Salvador, Bahia, on the southeastern shore of Brazil, a group of teenagers were gathered on the beach beneath the concrete wall supporting the city. Chattering in Portuguese and sharing cigarettes, the youngsters at first did not notice the cloudlike haze rising from the frothy sea in the darkness.

One of the boys in the group glanced out and saw the vague pale shape, but dismissing it as the crest of a long wave, turned to his friends again. Several minutes later, when he happened to look out at the water again, he realized the faint line was still there and getting closer.

"What *is* that?" he asked, pointing.

At first, the other teens paid him little mind. He repeated himself twice, then his companions began to follow his gaze out to sea. All conversation faded into silence, and as the group of youth watched in awe, shapes began to appear in the glowing haze. Dozens of ghostly heads rose out of the water, approaching them. Frozen in shock and fright, the teens watched as Passers emerged from the sea, migrating without speaking toward the land. They walked out of the surf and up the beach, passing through the concrete barrier and entering the city.

For several minutes after the Passers vanished, the young Brazilians looked at one another, mystified. Then they dashed off home to tell their parents what they'd seen.

CHAPTER 3

"Now this is an interesting case," said Dr. Ana deTarlo, tossing a thick manila file onto her wide fabricated desk. The man sitting across from her raised an eyebrow, then leaned forward to pick up the folder and open it. His Passer watched in the background.

Chester Williams was thirty-four and young for the influence he wielded as the leading voice in the country in *Passerism*, which along with *Passerist*, were terms he had coined for himself as an expert in the study of Passersby – or as they were commonly called, Passers. He did not take requests for medical consultations lightly, though he rarely reviewed them in person. That was what his assistants and affiliates were for. But the problem with a personal favor was that it had to be, well, personal.

He smacked his lips in mock patience as he read the information in the folder, his icy dark eyes skipping quickly through it. More than once, Williams had been referred to as a "punk" or "arrogant little twit" by his critics, and he had the looks and attitude to support their statements. He even seemed to embrace conflict.

"Why would you call this patient interesting?" he asked, his eyes still on the file. "I'm familiar with this name; I think St. Cross sent me information about this, but my people decided it was nothing and blew it off."

DeTarlo exhaled sharply as if in amused fortitude.

"Keep reading," she answered. She was at least fifteen years Williams's senior and had played no small role in building support for his reputation in the psychological field; she never let him forget it.

"Patient has been coming to the hospital with a variety of injuries and accidents for twelve years," Williams summarized aloud, looking up. "Each time claiming that a Passer was responsible and offering no other explanation. There have been dozens of cases like this since the Sentience began. It doesn't mean anything."

Dr. deTarlo stood up and bent over her desk, rudely snatching the file back out of his hand and plopping it open before her. The light from her lamp reflected off the clean white sheets and illuminated her face in the semi-gloom caused by the closed blinds on her window.

"What kind of an idiot do you think I am?" she snapped.

Williams smirked and sat back in his chair, tapping his fingertips on the end of the hard plastic armrest.

"You tell me. I didn't come all the way from Denver because I think that Fort Wayne is beautiful this time of year."

Ignoring his response, deTarlo explained, "Just days ago, this patient was admitted to the psych ward after a botched suicide attempt. Since then, he has suffered two more 'attacks'; the first time a phlebotomist was harmed in the process, and the

32

second time, another patient killed himself in the same room."

Williams arched an eyebrow, but didn't speak.

"Sounds like a typical dangerous psych patient, I know," Ana continued. "But the phlebotomist was adamant that the patient was 'being attacked.' She claims to have received injuries from the Passer involved, the one the patient identifies as 'Rubin,' though no spirits were visible at the time."

There was a flicker of recognition in Chester's eyes, though he said nothing.

"During the second attack," said deTarlo, "the patient began seizing and bleeding from the mouth, at one point asphyxiating. When the nurses and orderlies attempted to revive him, the defibrillator malfunctioned and has been examined and shows signs of electromagnetic radiation."

That caught Chester's notice and both eyebrows went up. He remained motionless in his chair but appeared to pay closer attention.

"Also strange is that no injuries were found to the patient's chest, heart, lungs, stomach, anything. The bleeding eventually stopped, but a source wound couldn't be found. A significant amount of hemorrhaging occurred, yet there was no internal bleeding. He was covered in bruises and scratches, but no actual incisions."

She paused to let the information sink in, and Williams began to lose interest again.

He began derisively: "Unless you pulled some strings to get me a doctorate without me knowing it…"

"I want to know about similar cases," deTarlo snapped.

"You could have just had one of my interns look it up for you."

"I don't want a list. I want to *know* about the attacks."

Chester remained still and looked at her for several moments as if waiting for an incentive, though his eyes glazed in thought.

"Dozens of cases at the beginning," he started finally. "Less through the years, mostly because they were false and general bad opinion did nothing for attention seekers. Two dozen cases in the last twenty years has dwindled to less than half that in the last decade. Last I was up to date on the information, there have been only two—well, three now—recorded cases of possible legitimate Passer harassment in the country in the past six months."

"Only *three*?" DeTarlo looked incredulous.

"That's the possible *legit* cases," Williams repeated. "I don't suppose I need to tell you that it's down to one where we thought there were none."

DeTarlo appeared confused, so Williams clarified. "Case one, a woman, killed herself in Detroit over a month ago. Case two just stabbed himself to death in your psych ward. This one, case three, is all that's left."

"You appear awfully nonchalant about putting these pieces together, Chet."

Williams narrowed his inky eyes at the nickname.

"Coincidences like this happen so often they become the norm," he said. "I get so much information about these things, it's no surprise to me anymore. The Passers have called in all debts with fate, and the world has become more balanced and symmetrical. You'd be surprised how much the

34

natural and spiritual worlds mirror one another when you really get into the facts and figures. Behavior aside, that is. Since when are you interested in Passer hunts?"

Ana tried to hide a smile and turned her eyes down to the file in front of her again.

"I haven't treated anyone with claims to this extent," she responded with a blasé shrug.

"Uh-huh." Williams waited to hear more.

"You know my fondness for fringe research. I've never read any reports that supported this sort of circumstance definitively. It's advantageous that Dr. St. Cross has kept such careful and detailed reports, even if he *has* been overly secretive."

"Isn't it patient confidentiality or whatever?"

"Oh, is it?" Ana lifted her eyebrow, shadows cast on her forehead by the reflection of light off the papers before her, exaggerating the dark line above her eye. "You just told me he sent you this report."

Chester shrugged, adopting the casualness she had just abandoned.

"St. Cross is a slug, I guess," he said. "If that's what you want me to think. He *has* been annoying."

"Oh, I've told you what I want you to think." She smiled deeply. A glimmer of pride and interest twinkled in her eyes at the mention of something she was familiar with and expert in. She was no stranger to how Williams's mind worked.

Chester ignored her gloating and said as a disclaimer: "I would check and double-check that my statement about case three being the last one is correct. There's no way my sources and interns are one hundred percent accurate all the time. Just because these are the only *recorded* cases of

35

believable Passer harassment doesn't mean there aren't other cases out there that either aren't taken seriously or just aren't reported."

DeTarlo still appeared very proud of herself and began shuffling through paperwork on her desk.

"I want you to reread the file in detail, and the other two cases as well," she said. "Write up a statement and sign it."

A look of intense annoyance and disappointment contorted Williams's face.

"Oh gimme a break!" he exclaimed. "I have a life and responsibilities. I've got the whole of *A.S.M.* to deal with, and the riots, and I'm in the middle of getting another book through a final draft. I don't have the time to write out reports for you."

"Then have your interns write it," deTarlo answered, unflustered. "But make sure you sign and agree with it. If we play our cards right, this could be just what we need to finally get just the subject we need for your Kelly Road project."

Chester glared at the psychologist murderously, and his watching Passer began to shift tensely in the shadow cast by the open office door in the evening light. Ana was not intimidated.

"Yes, I know about it," she said. "Do you think I wouldn't hear about something like that just because you try to keep it all hush-hush? I know that St. Cross tried to connect these dots too, but he got nowhere."

She stepped around her desk and cupped her hand to Chester's cheek patronizingly. He slapped her away and got to his feet, whirling toward the door to leave.

36

"You'll have your stupid report," he snarled. "But there's no way in hell I'd let you have the reins at Kelly Road."

"It's not up to you," she replied, vaguely gloating. "I control the subject, and public curiosity is on my side. Passerism is a fad that's becoming stale and obsolete."

"While we remain among you," answered Williams's Passer, Rod, "the study and worship of our kind shall never be obsolete." Dressed in a light-colored dress shirt with the sleeves rolled up to his elbows, the ghost was a sharp-eyed brunette that looked no older than Chester.

"Yes, and you'll always be around, so long as people keep dying," deTarlo said with a dismissive wave of her hand.

Williams slammed her office door behind him as he left, and Rod passed through it to follow.

Aidriel tensely tapped his bare foot against the floor and rubbed at his eyes with his fingertips.

"I have no advocate, then," he said grimly.

Dr. deTarlo crossed her legs at the knees, smoothing her pencil skirt. She leaned back in the plastic chair and rolled her eyes when it creaked.

"Why would you say that?" she smoothly asked, controlling her expression again.

Aidriel dropped his hands to his knees and eyed her before rising to pace in front of the window.

"Mr. Akimos," the psychologist began when he didn't answer. "You are under my supervision until I am satisfied you are no longer a danger to yourself or others. But you attacked a medical worker and are under investigation for a man's death."

She bobbed her head once in the direction of the orderly standing just inside the door, watching.

"Oh that's bullshit!" Aidriel exclaimed. "I was strapped down for Pete's sake. The man was tormented; he killed himself."

"Are you implying his suicide was the result of mental illness?"

"That's not what I meant," Aidriel snapped. "I mean he's dead because he couldn't take having to suffer the same way I am. He just managed actually offing himself."

"It's under investigation," deTarlo murmured.

Aidriel stared out the window at the horizon, shaking his head in disbelief, his hands on his hips.

"It's your decision, ultimately." Ana tried to keep her voice soothing. "You can either stay here or allow yourself to be transported to another, specialized facility."

"Bullshit," he said again. "If I say I want to stay locked in *this* prison cell, you'll come up with some medical gibberish reason that I'm not in my right mind and transport me anyway. I don't want any part of your stupid study."

DeTarlo pretended to be preoccupied with taking notes and didn't let his words register immediately.

"Why do you feel that way?" she asked without looking up.

Aidriel smiled bitterly and scratched at the back of his head. He knew the orderly was watching his every move like a hawk, and though the doctors had insisted he stay in bed, Aidriel just couldn't. He was getting stir-crazy.

"I didn't know this was about my feelings," he commented snippily.

"It's my job to evaluate your mental state."

"Last time I checked, I was still pretty sane."

"Then why did you attempt to take your own life?"

Aidriel exhaled deeply. For a brief moment he became very sad before pulling himself together.

"My mistake was botching something simple," he stated impassively. "No one ever wonders how long I can put up with this. I've been trying to convince everyone for twelve years that I'm serious and this is real, but you just ignore it. You're all wasting time trying to figure it out, but no one's *that* unlucky."

"Have you told Chester Williams?"

Aidriel snorted a laugh and shifted dangerously, watching the orderly out of the corner of his eye. It bothered him that he was being physically watched by the man while mentally monitored by the woman. St. Cross didn't play these games with him.

"Oh sure, your average fool can get personal meetings with the likes of Williams any day," he commented. Before deTarlo could make a patronizing reply, Aidriel walked over to the bed and sat on it with his back to her.

"There's no point in delaying the inevitable," he said grimly. "You're going to move me to your 'special facility' sooner or later. I've had all I can take of this place anyhow."

Dr. deTarlo got up and came to stand next to him, holding out her pen and clipboard.

"Sign these," she ordered, and he wordlessly complied.

"I want Dreamer there," he said, handing back the pen.

"Who?"

"The girl from the lab. I want her to be wherever I'm going."

She'd been on his mind often since the attack, and though he'd asked, they wouldn't let him see her. For her safety, they said. But he wanted to talk to her. If only to apologize, though he felt she could relate with him now. She'd be someone he could confide in with complete honesty, and she might even help him.

"Why?" DeTarlo didn't bother to hide her incredulity.

Aidriel looked up at her darkly.

"'Cause *she'll* believe me," he answered.

CHAPTER 4

The orderly behind Aidriel held the handles of the wheelchair in a death grip, his focus completely on the patient as he pushed him toward the ambulance bay doors. Through the glass panels, the two men could see Dr. deTarlo and a nurse motioning with their arms for visitors to stay away from the building. The few people nearby stepped back to watch and wait obediently, while the Passers remained wherever they were standing, their ghostly forms like clumps of fog in the early morning light. They were far enough away that they didn't appear to notice Aidriel, but he could see them. He sat frozen, his eyes unblinking, his attention focused on his senses, waiting for even the slightest sign he was going to be attacked. Besides his heart pounding like a dynamo, he was fine.

Eventually deTarlo was satisfied everything outside was under control. She stepped back through the doors anxiously and motioned for the orderly to bring Aidriel out to a waiting ambulance.

"I'm kind of surprised," the patient commented to the shrink as she fell into step beside him.

"Really, at what?"

"I figured you'd want to walk me straight out into a mob of Passers to see what would happen."

To Aidriel's astonishment, deTarlo nodded in genuine agreement.

"That option crossed my mind," she answered. "But Williams didn't think it was a good idea, what with the way the electromagnetic radiation would affect the ambulance."

She sounded serious; Aidriel was speechless.

Reaching the open back of the van, he got up from the chair and climbed in.

"Lie down," deTarlo ordered, pointing at the cot to one side. The EMTs staffing the vehicle kept their lips sealed and watched Aidriel for a reaction.

"What?" he asked, annoyed. "Why?"

"Do as I say," the shrink answered coolly, taking a seat on the bench.

Aidriel sat down on the stretcher and plopped onto his back. The EMTs strapped him in and hovered nearby attentively, as if expecting him to stop breathing at any moment.

Aidriel's intuitive sense of warning kicked in and pounded. The orderly took his time returning the wheelchair to the building before he hopped into the back of the van, pulling the doors closed. They waited without speaking, listening to the rumbling of the engine, and Aidriel prayed it wouldn't suddenly stall.

Eventually the vehicle began to move, and deTarlo insisted the siren be turned on.

"We're transporting a high-risk patient."

No one noticed the vague, sour smile on Aidriel's face.

"How're you feeling?" deTarlo asked him. "I'm sure you're more excited than I am."

"You aren't looking forward to the personal attention of Chester Williams and his staff?"

Aidriel didn't reply, but he was thinking that Williams's staff was probably half Passers. They had to be, with the work he did.

The drive went remarkably quickly with the lights and sirens, and soon they found themselves at the airport. Aidriel was itching to get off the cot and was up and moving as soon as the EMTs undid the straps.

"We're at the helipad," deTarlo told him. "This is where the chopper comes to drop off patients to the plane for transport. There aren't many people around. Less Passers."

The orderly opened the back doors and Aidriel peered out into the bright morning sunshine. He could see a private jet parked some ways off on a runway as he and the psychologist climbed out of the ambulance. Printed on the side of the aircraft was *American Sentience Movement* in bold, scrolly letters.

"Everything from here on out is run by Williams," deTarlo explained, taking his arm and leading him toward the plane as if he were a child. Aidriel resisted the urge to pull away, though he found it distracting to be hustled by a woman in pumps toward a plane. It made him feel like a fugitive being smuggled out of the country.

Earlier that morning, deTarlo had brought him regular street clothes to wear in place of the featureless dress of the psych ward. He was glad to have the jeans, sneakers and button-up shirt, but the dog tag was a bit much. It had his name and

43

medical record number on it, *Dr. Ana deTarlo, Psy.D.* and her contact number, along with the logo of Williams's company.

"Great, just in case I didn't already feel like a research subject," he'd complained.

"Just put it on," deTarlo had snapped irritably. "Why do you have to whine about everything? You should count yourself fortunate *American Sentience* is funding all of this and showing so much interest in you."

While he slipped the chain over his head, Aidriel had asked, "So why are *you* showing such an interest?"

"I won't lie," she'd said. "There has never been a case like yours since the Sentience began. With an expert like Williams involved, this study can be very beneficial for my career."

Aidriel had not known how to reply at first, and fingered the dog tag thoughtfully.

"What is the expected outcome of this 'study'?" he'd wanted to know.

DeTarlo had stared coldly as if he were just another case and wasn't waiting for her answer.

"I don't think that's information I have to discuss with you," she'd retorted. "You signed the consent forms. Once the report is published, feel free to read it."

Now, as the psychologist was dragging him toward the plane, Aidriel was starting to get cold feet. No one knew where he was or where he was going, and he wished he'd thought of someone to tell before they left. Did it really matter in the long run? He had a few friends and acquaintances, but what difference would it make if they knew where he was? Nobody would come after him. He thought

44

briefly of Dr. St. Cross, but he had stopped contact with his former shrink shortly after he saw him last and realized he didn't mind.

Aidriel also had reasons of his own to allow these bigwigs to shuffle him around like a curiosity to study. Since the attacks began, he had been unable to leave Indiana, and was curious to see if he ever could. Every time he'd tried, a Passer somehow blocked his way. He was always harmed in the process, and found himself waking up in the emergency room to the faces of confused doctors. He had mentioned this to deTarlo the morning before they left, but she hadn't appeared concerned or even convinced.

"I've tried to leave the state four times," Aidriel had explained. "Twice by car, once by motorcycle, once on foot. I met resistance every time."

"Uh-huh." Ana was busy overseeing the physical examination required for his discharge, and was looking over the doctor's shoulder at his chart. The medical intern had cast questioning glances at Aidriel, but was under strict orders to examine only and ignore any and all conversation.

"Look, it's in my record," Aidriel'd pressed on. "The second time by car, I was coming around a hairpin turn on a very steep embankment, and Rubin was standing in the road. I drove right through him and he killed the engine and punctured both the tires on the passenger side. I flew right off the cliff and was unconscious for fifteen hours."

"Quiet, please," the doctor'd said, placing a stethoscope against Aidriel's back, making him jump. DeTarlo couldn't look less interested in what Aidriel was saying, and was scribbling on her own clipboard, carefully examining the scars present on his body in comparison to those already recorded in his file.

"Way to feel like an object," he'd muttered.

"Quiet, please," the doctor repeated, moving the cold metal head of the stethoscope. "Deep breaths."

"We aren't traveling by car, Mr. Akimos," Ana said finally without looking up. "Williams is providing a private jet for us."

"That's what I'm afraid of," he'd mumbled.

As they neared the jet, Chester Williams came down the steps to meet them in a sports jacket and jeans. He looked very smart from a distance, but upon getting closer, Aidriel saw that the Passerist had studs in his ears and rings and bracelets on his hands and wrists. Though he was older than Aidriel, he reminded the patient of his younger years, before he realized jewelry was painful to remove from injured limbs.

"Dr. deTarlo," Williams said without smiling, nodding his head once.

"Chet," Ana responded with a smirk. Chester glanced at Aidriel and looked him up and down, but did not address him.

"Where is his tag?" he asked the shrink.

Without speaking, Aidriel pulled the object in question out from under his shirt and swung it up and down by its chain with a belittling look on his face. Williams saw it and turned away, leading them back up the stairs to the jet.

Dr. Ana deTarlo was the only person Aidriel knew from the hospital on the plane. He'd hoped to see Dreamer and wondered when and if he ever would again. Chester had his own crew of security and private orderlies in black scrubs with the *American Sentience Movement* logo on their chest pockets. One of them forcibly plunked Aidriel into a seat then leaned over him to secure his belt. He decided these guys were more like medical mercenaries than actual orderlies, and smiled slightly. There wasn't a single Passer in sight, but Aidriel kept aware, hoping the uneasiness in his stomach was just because he was nervous.

"I've made sure there aren't any Passers in the vicinity," he heard Williams tell deTarlo. "But to tell you the truth, if we don't have any problems, that could mean this whole thing is a waste of time."

"We won't talk about this," the psychologist rudely hushed him. "You don't have the right to doom this project before it has even begun."

It surprised Aidriel that deTarlo could speak so insolently to Williams when she had led him to believe the Passerist was in charge of all of this. Chester glared at Ana but didn't answer, pushing past her to take a seat across a table from Aidriel. DeTarlo walked toward the front of the plane and spoke softly with a man and a woman in lab coats, probably doctors.

For several moments, Williams regarded Aidriel with cold dark eyes, his face set in a serious frown that gave him the appearance of a rebel. The patient waited quietly; it wasn't his place to speak first.

47

"You probably think," said Chester finally, "that I am your enemy here. Because I am an advocate and ambassador to the Passers, that I'll do everything in my power to prove you a fraud."

Aidriel didn't bother to say that the thought had crossed his mind, and simply allowed his eyebrows to arch.

Williams glanced out the small round window of the plane and sucked his lower lip into his mouth between his teeth.

"There's never been a need to prove anyone a fraud," he said, releasing his lip with a smack. "There has never been evidence to support anyone's claim. Usually attention-seekers give up long before they are actually taken seriously."

Aidriel shifted, briefly raising his eyebrows again and blinked, waiting for Williams to get to the point.

"There is no definiteness to any natural law," the Passerist continued. "The Passers were human once too. They cannot be entirely unlike us, and I'm looking for what faults they have in common with us."

"But the Passers have always *seemed* kind and protective," pointed out Aidriel in a low voice.

Chester cracked a half-smile and nodded.

"But there have always been liars."

Dr. deTarlo joined them and stood over Williams with one arm wrapped around her clipboard, balancing it on her hip.

"Chet, unless you're recording this conversation, you shouldn't be talking to my patient."

Without looking up, Chester raised his hand and gave her the middle finger.

"Stop acting like a child." DeTarlo was hardly moved, and maintained a patient, condescending tone.

Williams narrowed his eyes angrily and got swiftly to his feet so he stood face-to-face with the shrink.

"Let's get something cleared up," he hissed. "You are not my mother. Just because you and my father had an understanding doesn't mean I'm your little servant boy. You can't yank the medical permission you got for this, but I can sure as hell yank the funding. So get the hell off my back. Your gloating has passed the point of being tolerable."

Without waiting for her to respond, he pushed past her and stalked toward his chair near the front of the plane. DeTarlo took his vacated place across from Aidriel and secured her belt, a smirk of pride plastered on her face. Her cheeks were flushed, and she distractedly ran her fingers along her elaborately twisted hair to make sure nothing had come loose.

"Wheels up in five," she said neutrally.

Aidriel tilted his head back against the headrest. He held his breath and waited.

It surprised Aidriel that the flight and drive from the airport passed without incident. He remained tense and aware, but deTarlo found that amusing.

"Williams has made preparations for your transportation," she explained.

"Forgive me for not being more relaxed, then," he responded. "Though it isn't uncommon for me to make short trips every so often without being attacked."

"I'd imagine you'd be dead by now if that weren't the case," commented the shrink. "Of course, if you'd had your way, you would be."

It startled him how insensitively she'd brought up his suicide attempt, and, ignoring the burning stares of the orderlies riding with them, he glanced out the window of the van that had picked them up.

Kelly Road was a long stretch of gravel-paved country street that was too far from everything for buildings to be seen in any direction once the caravan of vehicles arrived at Williams's facility. The larger of the two fence-haloed structures was massive and unexpectedly plain on the outside, affording a single line of small windows to face the road on the first level alone. One side of the building was a two-story car garage that was already populated by several cars and SUVs when they arrived.

A second, small building sat across the street, shaped like a control tower at an airport. Outside the copious barriers, the compound was surrounded by nothing but crop fields, overgrown ditches and dense clumps of trees. They were still in the Midwest; the flight hadn't taken longer than an hour. No one would tell Aidriel what state they were even in, however.

Williams's car was at the front of the little procession, and paused at the security gate at the entrance of the lot. The driver rolled down his window, leaned out to exchange words with the security guard, then handed over a card. A moment later, he took the card back and the gate opened. Once the other vehicle had entered the compound, the van Aidriel and deTarlo were riding in pulled up and the driver went through the same motions. *Afternoon*s were exchanged, paperwork was checked, then the gate opened to allow them to drive in.

The vehicles had parked in the upper level of the garage and everyone got out. More medical mercenaries were waiting for them when they reached the bottom of the elevator. They'd brought a stretcher with them, and Aidriel glanced questioningly at deTarlo.

"Get on it and lie down," she ordered. Embarrassed that he was clearly capable of walking, Aidriel hesitated.

All eyes were on him, so he complied with the remark, "I don't know you *that* well."

The orderlies mirrored his awkward smile, but deTarlo acted as if she had not heard, and the joke passed without breaking any ice.

Once Aidriel was supine, the orderlies secured the familiar straps, but the group still did not start walking. A woman in black scrubs like the others, probably a nurse, drew some liquid into a syringe from a bottle and turned Aidriel's arm without speaking to him, rolling up his sleeve to insert the needle into the antecubital area inside his elbow.

"What's this for?" he asked deTarlo. She ignored him and was making more notes on her clipboard. It didn't take long for Aidriel to realize he'd been given a sedative. His eyelids got heavy and he started to drift off. He could feel the stretcher begin to move, but Ana's voice said, "Wait until he's completely unconscious before taking him inside."

51

"So he won't know the way to…?" one of the orderlies began to ask. Aidriel passed out before he could hear the rest.

The phlebotomist Dreamer and several members of the medical staff had arrived at Kelly Road the day before Aidriel did. They'd been assigned to featureless quarters with two beds a room and two rooms to a bathroom. It didn't take long for the phleb and her nurse roommate to unpack the single suitcase they'd each been allowed to bring. They were shown to their workstations and allowed time to access their supplies with the direction to fill out a request form if anything was missing.

Dreamer arranged her little cupboard to her liking then rearranged it again to pass the time. The nurses were clustering at their first aid closet, chatting and exchanging rumors about the true nature of their temporary employment. Bored and excluded, the phleb wandered off to explore and mostly found locked doors and offices crowded with paperwork and blank computer screens.

At the end of a hall on the ground floor was a pair of large double doors announcing *The Bird Cage*. The name was mysterious and intriguing, but the technicians and engineers pushing in and out of the entryway told her in passing that she should not go in without permission.

A voice over the intercom announced the arrival of Chester Williams and the "subject" while Dreamer was looking over the coffee and snack machines with passionless attention. She curiously wandered in the direction of the parking garage, falling into step with a nurse carrying a bottle of tranquilizer and a syringe on an errand for a doctor. As they neared the garage, the nurse told Dreamer not to come any further with her, though not impolitely, and the phleb obeyed. She was loitering in the hallway when the door opened again and Williams, deTarlo and their entourage passed by with Aidriel on a stretcher. Dreamer stood back and watched them hurry by, her eyes ever on their patient.

He looked a different man than the one she had met at the hospital. Peaceful and motionless, his rugged face was free of worry when he was not awake. She liked the boyish manliness of his appearance; she'd thought his voice and manner attractive from the first time she saw him. His eyes had depth and character behind the pain he couldn't hide. Incidentally, she'd heard him laugh bitterly in the psych ward and liked the sound. And his arms were to die for; lean and muscular and with veins that would make any phlebotomist swoon.

But the seriousness and preoccupation on the countenances of the group of important people escorting Aidriel sent chills through Dreamer. When she had received the offer—or rather, the demand—of employment by American Sentience Movement, she had hesitated only briefly, accepting on the promise in her mind of more interaction with the unsound patient from the 4th floor and more chances at eavesdropping on the fascinating mystery of his case.

Dreamer was young and had thought this would be a pleasant adventure. There was, however, no wide-eyed curiosity or optimistic hope on the faces of those few privileged with the true facts of the case. Even the strangeness of the constant company of the ghosts was still somehow ordinary. *This* was not the stuff of a superhero movie; Aidriel was only human and would be whatever those in authority over him wished him to be. Dreamer knew she was nothing also. She and Aidriel were just people, everyday intelligences and personalities that could be two anybodies passing each other on the street. They were not beautifully paranormal like the Passers; they were not rich or genius or talented like Williams and deTarlo and the other strange people so dark and unusual beneath the surface.

The phlebotomist got the feeling as the stretcher and its escort passed that something horrible had been happening in secret and would continue, against the irrelevant will of her conscience, in the clandestine room beyond the doors marked *The Bird Cage*.

"Mr. Akimos, speak when you understand me."

Aidriel's answer was a low groan, and he blinked in the hazy light. He could tell when he moved that he was lying on a comfortable cushion, and his arms touched soft, yielding surfaces on both sides. The notion that he might be cradled in some kind of tiny cocoon set off his fears of being smothered and he startled himself awake.

He was lying on his back on a wide bed surrounded with four walls of thick foam padding. It reminded him of a tiny padded cell.

Dr. deTarlo was standing to his right, a pen nestled between the fingers of her hand resting on the cushioning, her mouth a tight, straight line.

"You didn't come out easily," she said, clicking her pen, glancing at her watch, and recording the time on her clipboard. Aidriel didn't apologize. He was grateful for deep sleep, even if it was drug induced. Constant dread did not make for a restful night.

The psychologist unlocked and lowered the padding on one side just as if it were a hospital bed, and stepped back, ordering him to sit up. Aidriel's head felt like it weighed a hundred pounds, but he managed to drag himself into a sitting position and hold it upright.

They were inside a geodesic dome–shaped structure made of what looked like thick fogged glass with white light glowing through it. In addition to the bed, there was a bolted-down table and two swiveling chairs amid the heavily padded room that was akin to a fast-food restaurant. There was a couch, a television, and a closed-off cubicle with a shower and toilet. Three plastic storage tubs with lids were neatly piled to one side, opposite the bed and next to two translucent doors with padded crash bars.

"This is what we call the Bird Cage," Dr. deTarlo told him. "It's where you'll be living for the duration of the study. Cameras have been mounted in the framework of the structure, and you will be monitored via video, audio, and sensory equipment twenty-four hours a day."

"What am I supposed to do?" Aidriel asked groggily.

"It makes no difference to us what you do," responded Ana with an indifferent shrug. "We've been liberal enough to provide you mindless entertainment. There mustn't be any sound pollution, so the television is muted and subtitled. Books can be arranged."

She made vague motions in the direction of the TV as she spoke, adding, "Whatever you require, within reason, to give your life some impression of meaning."

Aidriel mused for a moment on his past life; the blurry memories not worth the space they occupied in his brain. The meaninglessness of work and paying bills and cleaning house, all without hope or satisfaction. If that painful cycle resumed, in the even more mind-numbing state deTarlo was describing, it wouldn't be long before he was again looking for a permanent way out.

"What about contact with the outside world?" he asked.

"Who would you want to contact?"

The question stung his pride, and Aidriel rubbed at the back of his neck, forgetting the still-sore bruises from his noose until he inflamed them.

"No one," he mumbled when she waited for his answer.

The psychologist set her mouth and nodded, turning to walk toward the doors.

"Wait, is Dreamer here, then?" Aidriel called after her.

"Yes."

"Can I see or talk to her?"

Ana spun around gracefully on her heel and peered at him over her tortoiseshell glasses.

"Why? So you can attack her again? Or is she your girlfriend?" she asked mockingly.

"No," he directly answered, though a flash of light in the periphery of his senses warmed him a little at the thought of answering an affirmative to her second question. The phlebotomist, whom he had built slowly up in his mind as a friend, an advocate, a kindred spirit, was, if only as he imagined her, a pleasant candidate for partnership. He pictured her going to bat for him to his critics at that very moment while he was unaware. He liked the look that he envisioned in her eyes when he told her everything; a look of complete acceptance, the total opposite of the disbelief and forbearance of all others he'd tried to persuade in the past.

Dr. deTarlo could tell by Aidriel's faraway expression that his mind had wandered, and she snorted, shaking her head.

It suddenly dawned on Aidriel that any façade of faux decency that deTarlo had worn earlier was gone. He had no idea where he was or how to get out, and with no contact with the outside, the chances of him leaving before they were done with him were nonexistent.

"I won't talk to anyone *but* her," he stated of Dreamer. He was reaching for some semblance of control over his situation. Dr. deTarlo just smiled.

"Who says you need to say anything?" she asked, strutting once more toward the exit. Aidriel was too dazed to move or speak. He watched the shrink step through the doors into the darkness beyond, and heard them slam shut and mechanically lock behind her.

****

57

Sessions used to be different with Dr. St. Cross than they were with deTarlo. Ana was more interested in data than what her patient was thinking or feeling, but St. Cross was different. He would listen to what Aidriel said, and usually offer some advice more direct than Aidriel had thought customary of shrinks.

"Describe yourself in five words," St. Cross once said.

Aidriel responded, "Cursed."

"That's only one," pointed out St. Cross.

"Someone who is definitely cursed," tried Aidriel.

"I'm talking about what's inside," the psychiatrist explained. "What you feel like."

Aidriel said, "Tired."

St. Cross added, "Cynical."

"Smothered," continued Aidriel.

"Yet isolated," finished the doctor. "See? That's five words."

Aidriel had made a face and shrugged.

"Not a pretty picture, though."

"Don't feel sorry for yourself," St. Cross advised him. "No one is to blame for your troubles. Take responsibility for your life and make it better."

"The Passers are to blame," Aidriel corrected him.

"Do you think that is a legitimate excuse? Do you think you can go through your life blaming everything on someone else, even if they're dead?"

"My life probably won't be long anyway, so why not?"

Aidriel had often resisted what St. Cross would recommend, at least in appearance. Studying the

58

spines of the books lined up on the doctor's shelf by the window gave him something to do while stonewalling the shrink.

"That's a coward's excuse for troubles," St. Cross had told him. "Are you a coward, Aidriel?"

"Yes," Aidriel replied defiantly.

"And is that the Passers' fault too?"

Aidriel didn't respond.

"Grow up," said St. Cross, his words harsher than his tone. "Stop acting like a rebellious child. You're wasting my time, and more importantly, your own. I think you are keenly aware of how much you value your own time and resources. Are you going to let yourself be run over? Are you just going to give up and sit down in the road?"

"That might be the best thing to do," countered Aidriel, level-toned despite the lecture.

"Perhaps *sometimes* it is, but not now."

"What am I supposed to do about it?"

"*Nothing* if you don't care. Fall over dead, if you want."

The look of agreement on Aidriel's face seemed to give St. Cross pause, and he'd changed his tactic.

"You need a kick in the pants, alright," he said, "but biting sarcasm is clearly not the correct foot. You think you're helpless, but you're not. There is no literal chain around your leg, no literal prison walls on all sides. Fight until you are entirely incapable of fighting anymore. You'll either die trying, the possibility of which you don't seem to mind, or you'll triumph."

"Or my legs will get yanked out from under me," stated Aidriel dully, "and I'll fall flat on my face, still alive and broken."

"If you don't try to fight," said St. Cross, "your legs'll get yanked out from under you, alright. *I'll* be the one doing the yanking."

St. Cross was serious in his belief that everything possible should be done to support his patients' efforts to help themselves, but Aidriel had ignored him. He'd chosen to attempt the "fall over dead" route, and it had gotten him into a different mess.

CHAPTER 5

Even the television station was too controlled for Aidriel to tell the time of day or the date. He guessed from the commercials that they were in Pennsylvania or Eastern Ohio. There was no guide to what would be airing, and no way of keeping track of the hours based on the programming. They'd taken his watch away while he was in the hospital and he hadn't gotten it or any of his other personal belongings back. The storage tubs contained clean clothing for him, and he had only the pair of shoes he was wearing when he arrived.

Every so often, at intervals he couldn't consider a schedule because they were purposefully erratic, the door would open and three of the medical mercenaries would come in. He had been given an electronic reading device with a random selection of books on it, and was fed twice a day. There were five bland meals they cycled through at random, ignoring the fact he hated the fish and never touched it. The water tasted like minerals, and barely took the edge off his perpetual thirst. He was used to some degree of paranoia, but since arriving at the Bird Cage he'd been increasingly agitated or overwhelmingly drowsy, even dizzy, which he attributed to boredom and being sedentary. The orderlies did not seem to consider him a threat and didn't bother to talk to him. What was there to say?

"How many days have I been here?" Aidriel finally asked when he was sure a full week had passed. "I need to know how long I've been in one place."

The orderlies raised their eyebrows at him like he was a monkey trying to imitate them, and left without answering his question.

If only each day were indeed his last. Living as if there might be no tomorrow caused every minute to pass at an agonizingly slow rate, and Aidriel was itching for something to happen. He began to ache for a rope and a branch to hang it from, and he was almost impatient for what he knew was going to occur, though he dreaded it also.

"I have to know how long I've been here!" Aidriel called out to the ceiling, unsure of where the cameras or sensors even were. "I *need* to know how long it's been."

Time was important. He had to know how long it would be before the Passers would find him.

After the first meal on one of the featureless days, Aidriel was sitting at the table with his chin resting on his folded arms when the doors unlocked and Dreamer came in with two orderlies as an escort.

"Hi, I'm here to draw some blood," she said as if they were strangers.

Without speaking, Aidriel straightened and pulled up his sleeve, extending his arm. His face let slip the smallest sign of his pleasure at finally seeing her and his hopes that she might be all he imagined she was. Dreamer set her tray of supplies on the table, but one of the mercenaries picked it up again to keep it out of Aidriel's reach.

"Why does my blood have to be tested?" Aidriel asked. "Am I on drugs?"

Dreamer wouldn't look at him or answer, but took a small sheet of labels for the tubes from her tote. Pretending to double-check the stickers, she laid them on the table, tapping them with her fingertip to draw Aidriel's attention to a certain word. The labels were upside-down, but in the snatch of view Aidriel had before one of the orderlies picked up the sheet he saw the word *Depakene*. He had no idea what that was and looked to the phlebotomist, who had chosen her supplies from the tray and was putting on her gloves. She mouthed the word "schizophrenia."

The orderly with the labels cleared his throat; Dreamer ignored him, tying her tourniquet around Aidriel's arm, choosing the sight and cleansing it with an alcohol wipe while Aidriel watched her closely for any other subtle communication. She went about her business without talking at first, finally warning just before the needle pierced his skin, and waiting while the red-and-yellow-topped tube filled.

Her casual silence gave Aidriel the impression that he had not been privy to the obvious fact the two of them were somehow as thick as thieves. Dreamer sneaked a glance at him and smiled a little; he admitted to himself that she had been on his mind often since their shared attack. She was wearing short-sleeved scrubs, and he could see the barely perceptible shadows on her right arm of the

63

injuries she had received during the attack. They had corresponding tattoos of sorts.

"What's going on outside?" Aidriel murmured. He turned his gray eyes up at her, and she glanced at the mercenaries before answering; they didn't motion or speak.

"A whole lot of nothing," Dreamer said. "Dr. deTarlo is angry with Mr. Williams all the time, and as far as any of us med workers know, none of our Passers will come here."

"Why?"

"I don't know, but even Mr. Williams's Passer is shunning him."

"Sounds like a stressful working environment."

Dreamer smiled slightly before she could stop herself. She took a short breath as if to speak, but didn't.

"I'm at their mercy here," Aidriel whispered, turning his wrist so he could grip her elbow. The phleb hesitated, then undid the tourniquet, leaning closer as she did so.

"Rubin showed up last night," she murmured. "It's been standing outside, waiting."

Aidriel cursed under his breath. Dreamer was finished with her draw, but as she removed the needle, she intentionally lifted it enough to widen the puncture wound. Her intention was to cause more bleeding to allow a few more moments in his company. If it hurt, Aidriel showed no sign of it.

"They can hear everything we're saying," she told him while she held gauze to the wound. "I don't know if you can speed this 'project' along enough to be freed, but is there something you know that we don't?"

Aidriel took his time answering as if he had to think.

"Rubin's not waiting for me," he said. "If it hasn't come in yet, it's because it's waiting for others."

"Other what?"

"Other Passers."

"This dome is an electromagnetic field. You'll be—"

"I might as well be standing in the middle of the street," Aidriel said definitively. "You can't hide from them."

Rubin had always been around. Aidriel could remember, as a boy, standing at the end of the driveway watching his father's truck vanish around the far curve in the road, never to return. Rubin was nearby, observing also.

"You have your mother," the Passer had told him. "She loves you, and your father only disciplined you. I'll do that now."

It was not an idle threat, and for the rest of Aidriel's childhood, he was slapped or reprimanded almost daily by Rubin for getting out of line. He fell into a cycle of forced trust with the Passer, relying on the dead older man's opinion of balance to keep the peace. His mother had other things on her mind, and didn't interfere. It suited her just fine that her only son didn't get into trouble and treated her with respect.

The relationship between boy and ghost was not only a violent one, though. Rubin had been deceased for more than a century. It was tolerant of listening to troubles and freely offered advice.

65

"What did you die of?" young Aidriel had once asked.

"I was a rich man," Rubin told him, calling attention to the garish red velvet vest it always wore. "I lived long enough ago that I could own slaves and had workers to maintain my extensive grounds. My life was long and comfortable, but I was not generous, and I died of food poisoning after an extravagant feast honoring my birthday."

"What is it like to have so much money and power?" starry-eyed Aidriel had wanted to know.

"Find out for yourself," Rubin said.

"Does that mean that someday I will be rich?"

"I don't tell lies."

"But is that what you meant?"

"Stop questioning me, child," Rubin responded testily.

"But you can see the future. I want to know."

Rubin had cuffed Aidriel and left him alone.

As Aidriel entered his teens, the physical punishments lessened, but the advice and companionship did also. Rubin was still often present. However, it began to act more and more as if it resented Aidriel. When he was seventeen, Aidriel finally learned why.

"I'm going to kill you," Rubin had said.

Aidriel was breathless and barely managed to ask why.

"I hate you," responded the Passer. "We all do. I've lost years' worth of opportunities to kill you. Be sure that I will accomplish it, though."

Aidriel could remember his father threatening to kill him once. The elder Akimos had not made good on his promise, electing instead to leave. Rubin, however, was not his father.

****

It was both boring and calming to supervise the video, audio and electromagnetic data feed from the Bird Cage. A group of technicians took shifts sitting in front of the cluster of four screens in the monitor room, watching with half of their attention while focusing the rest on a book or a football game on a small TV. Once or twice a day, Chester Williams would come into the room for an update.

"There's been a lot of static and flashing in and out on the video feed," the tech on duty told him on one such visit during the second week. "Nothing but blurs and temperature clouds on the thermal, but there's been distinct interference on the other two feeds."

"Show me," ordered Williams, leaning on his fist on the desk. The technician consulted a list of times he'd recorded in a log notebook, scrolling to the corresponding frames on the monitor.

The first time frame listed showed a strange foggy shape flash in front of Camera Number 2 for only four or five frames. The tech slowed it down, and Chester peered at the screen. It took him several seconds to realize it was a ghostly hand trying to block the camera.

People were used to seeing Passers living among them by now. It wasn't strange or frightening to view a crowd and perceive that half of the faces were translucent. They weren't misshapen; the cause of death was not visible on the spirit of a vacated body. But to witness a Passer in a way that ghosts used to be seen before the Sentience, in sinister snatches or threatening poses, made Chester shudder.

The disturbing images continued. In the footage, Aidriel wandered aimlessly from one resting place to another, doing very little to extricate himself from a trance, but all around him was ghostly activity. The technician showed Williams video frame after frame of Passers blocking the cameras or flashing terrible expressions of hatred or agony of which Aidriel was completely, possibly intentionally, oblivious.

Chester recognized one of the Passers' faces. He saw for several seconds that while Aidriel had his back turned, a ghost made itself visible several paces behind him, and stood absolutely still, watching him. When he began to turn around, it vanished. It was Williams's own spirit companion, and seeing it standing in such an attitude that he had never seen before sent chills down his spine.

"I don't want to see any more," Chester said.

"There's audio feedback too," said the technician. "Only one mike would pick it up at a time, so it's most likely Electronic Voice Phenomena."

Once more consulting his notations, the tech scrolled through the audio files until he reached a certain time, playing the clip for Williams. At first there was simply soft white noise, the amplified scraping sound of Aidriel moving, then a fuzzy, distorted voice clearly saying, "I bring death."

The tech ran it over twice more, and Chester rubbed at his eyes with his thumb and middle finger. The dim light in the room and seemingly cold temperature only magnified his sense of unfounded fear, a feeling he hadn't had since watching movies about haunted houses as a child.

The next audio file played was similar in its arrangement. White noise, movement sounds from Aidriel, then a very quiet voice that gave a long wheeze and hissed, "Be gone! Curses!"

"That's enough," Williams said before the tech could play anything more. "I get the picture."

"Then here's the printout of the electromagnetic fluctuations," the other man summed up, handing over a pile of several pages showing numbers, waving lines, and technical data. Chester looked over the information briefly, taking it in and pondering it while glancing around at the screens.

Aidriel was sitting quietly at the table with his head on his arm; he often assumed this position. The image appeared frozen on the monitors, and lulled Williams into a near- blindness as his mind worked and his eyes barely registered what they were seeing. The fright that washed over him all of a sudden made the hair on his arms and neck stand up. The tech caught his breath; he had seen it too.

For the briefest of moments, a Passer had appeared inside the Bird Cage, taking several steps toward Aidriel before it became invisible again. Chester realized he was trembling as he stared unblinking at the video feed, waiting with bated breath to see if the Passer would make itself perceptible again. For several seconds, the image did not change.

"Can *you* see it, sir?" whispered the tech. Williams shook his head. He would be able to see the Passer in its invisible state if he were in the Bird Cage with it, but the ghost was at present in a plane that the video cameras could not detect; even the thermal imaging feed from Camera Number 1 showed nothing.

Something might happen; even at a run, Chester wouldn't be able to reach the dome in less than ten minutes. There were doors to unlock and stairs to navigate, if he circumvented the maddeningly slow elevator. He didn't want to take the chance of leaving the room and missing an appearance on camera of the Passer.

"Should we alert security?" breathed the tech.

Without answering, Chester held up his hand to signal patience. He was frozen, staring at the screen where the Passer was visible again. It stood just across the table from Aidriel, who did not stir. His back rose and fell with slow regularity; he was most likely asleep, and wouldn't see the attack coming before it was too late.

But as Williams and the tech watched, holding their breath, they saw the Passer turn slowly around and walk away from Aidriel, nearly reaching the wall of the Bird Cage before it vanished.

For several seconds, Chester and the tech silently tried to calm themselves, relieved that nothing had happened. Both were startled out of their wits when the same Passer they had just seen suddenly appeared again, flying up at Camera 4 with a horrifying expression, its eye sockets black as holes, shrieking a spine-chilling scream. With echoing cries of fear, the two men jumped back from the console, and Williams fled in a panic, leaving the poor tech, ashen with terror, to stare at the screen, where the lens on Camera 4 was obscured by three deep nail scratches.

****

Whoever had designed the Bird Cage had not seemed concerned with simulating the change of light between night and day, but Aidriel could tell the difference. He'd sit for hours in the chair at the table, sometimes drifting off to sleep with his head on his arm. Vague shadows would begin to backdrop the furniture and the lights above, and he would know night was falling. He observed the changing of time this way after being suddenly awakened by what he, in a state of half-consciousness, thought was a shriek, and he began to become agitated.

The familiar sense of pain and nausea gripped the pit of his stomach, and he had the desperate urge to run. There was nowhere to run to, nowhere to hide.

The dome began to hum faintly; perhaps the electromagnetic field had been increased. Outside of it, he heard the echo of footsteps, voices, ragged breathing. Rubin was here, and was probably not alone.

Aidriel got up and walked to the wall near the doors, touching the pane to feel its temperature, peering through it into the gloom. The warmth of the surface began to noticeably drop, and Aidriel was startled to see Rubin suddenly step up close to the glass, though it stayed outside. Its hand came toward him, its long sharp nails scratching noisily on the dome's exterior.

Taking several paces back, Aidriel looked around and saw the ghostly silhouettes of dozens of Passers standing just outside the Bird Cage, watching, waiting. Rubin continued to wheeze and scrape at the pane.

The ringing in Aidriel's ears changed pitch and he fled from the wall, moving to the middle of the open floor. He didn't want to be near any of the furniture, even if it was padded. He didn't want to be smothered. Sitting down Indian-style, he leaned forward as far as he could, wrapping his arms around his head.

"This won't keep them out," he whispered despairingly.

Rubin's breathing stopped; he shrieked and the other Passers screamed out as well. Aidriel could hear the television sputter, hiss and explode with a spray of sparks, then the Passers were upon him. Dozens of hands tore at his clothing and hair, nails digging into his flesh and pulling, scratching, gouging. Their screams were deafening, and, folded so tightly against them, Aidriel couldn't breathe. The pain was unbearable and crushing, but he was too much in shock to cry out.

One of the Passers grabbed onto a handful of his hair and pulled hard, coming away with a chunk that it flung away in disgust, reaching for more. Hands were seizing and pulling Aidriel from all sides. One overwhelmed the others, dragging him by his shoulder several feet toward the wall before losing its grip. Another kicked him hard in the neck, and for a few seconds he blacked out. He barely had a chance to cough and suck in a breath before another clamped its claws over his face, trying to smother him.

There had to be dozens of them, swarming like a shapeless cloud of misty wasps all stinging at once. Aidriel's shoes and socks were yanked off, his feet trampled and punctured. Pieces of his clothing were being cut and ripped away, the exposed flesh falling target to the flying claws. Some of the Passers have paranormal weapons and were stabbing or hitting him. Clifford was there among them, using his scissors to strike with the same hatred and ferocity as Rubin.

Aidriel was seized and dragged toward the wall again, his hand groping desperately at the carpet before it was stomped and kicked. A female Passer shoved his head back with both hands, tipping him backward and sitting down on his chest, gripping his throat to strangle him. A male was twisting his leg, trying to dislocate it at the knee, and Rubin was striking at his face with both fists.

Unable to breathe or think, Aidriel instinctively tried to block the blows or fight back, his blotchy vision focused on Rubin. It was at times like these that all memories of his Passer being kind vanished. Aidriel couldn't recall anything about any other spirits before they chose to hate him, though he was not so young when it began that he could forget.

Clifford shoved the strangling woman aside and took its place, swinging the scissors down swiftly, striking a different location each time. It seemed to Aidriel that Rubin and Clifford's heads passed through each other and combined for a moment; his vision was exaggerating the translucent effect of the spirits as his brain was starved of oxygen. He remembered what Clifford had told him—that he was the last one. The burden had been passed and multiplied; never before had he been attacked so viciously or by so many.

Aidriel was grabbed by his outstretched arm again and jerked swiftly sideways, away from the wall. He slid out from under some of the Passers, though others managed to hang on. Tangible hands were holding him; Williams and two orderlies had arrived and were trying to get him out of the swarming pass of murderous ghosts.

"Rod, stop it!" Chester yelled at one of the male spirits. Williams began cursing and threw himself over Aidriel's body, ineffectually endeavoring to block the raging hands. The orderlies continued to drag their limp patient across the floor on his back, their eyes darting around in confusion as to what was happening. The strangling female was splattering blood at them and shrieking in rage, her swipes having no effect. Even Williams appeared untouched by the Passers, but there was no denying the spirits were there.

Rod and Rubin were frothing at the mouth, digging their claws into Aidriel's sides and pulling against the orderlies. Clifford swung his scissors at Chester but missed. The ethereal blades struck Aidriel in the side of the head, flooding his mouth and ear with blood. He was finally beginning to lose consciousness from the pain and asphyxiation and could do nothing in his defense. He felt his body leave the floor as the tug-of-war became more intense. The ghost gripping his leg continued to twist it sharply to try to cause the knee to dislocate, but the white hot flashes of pain in Aidriel's nerves caused a reflexive kick that succeeded in flinging the spirit away.

Chester's smartphone exploded in his pocket; he recoiled in surprise, his grip slipping. The Passers wrenched Aidriel away and dragged him all the way over to the wall, striking his head and shoulder against it as if they had forgotten he couldn't be hauled through. It didn't stop the hate-filled spirits from continuing their attack, though here and there, they were losing steam and fading away into nothing one at a time.

Rubin punched Aidriel in the chest as hard as it could but he managed to get a breath in. Williams and the orderlies seized him once more, pulling as hard and swiftly as they could, and freeing him from most of the ghostly hands. The Passers no longer touching him yelled out in disappointment and vanished, but a few hangers-on refused to give up fighting. Clifford got in one more stab then disappeared. Rod was flexing its nails in Aidriel's shoulder, screaming in a cursing match with Chester. Rubin gripped Aidriel by the throat, choking him senseless, but suddenly released and drifted back away from the struggle as if it had deployed an invisible parachute. As soon as it had given up in the attack, the other Passers did as well; within a moment, all of them were gone.

With moans of exhaustion, Williams and the orderlies dropped Aidriel to the floor and slumped down beside him. Their patient was unconscious and a bloody, battered mess. One of the orderlies was shaking violently, looking at the blood all over his chest and hands and trying to wipe it off.

"I need a drink," muttered the other in a thick Southern accent.

Chester crawled to Aidriel, leaning over him and checking for a pulse.

"Still breathing," he panted, crouching back down on his haunches. He fished his phone out of his pocket and dropped it, shaking his hand to ease the sudden burn caused by touching the electronic device. The phone was melted and smoking.

"Is that from the Bird Cage's field?" asked the Southern orderly. Williams shook his head.

Dr. Ana deTarlo was pacing up and down the hallway in the office area, her heels clicking and screeching as she turned on them swiftly. Some half-wit designer had chosen to display large photographs of tropical scenes on the walls between the doors. Not that the psychologist had anything against the tropics, but it seemed so inappropriate for the facility that it came off as tacky.

The double doors to the medical wing flew open with such force they slammed into the walls on either side. Williams came stalking out, putting on a clean sport jacket, two security guards and an assistant following a step behind him.

DeTarlo stepped aside and let Chester go by, falling into his procession between him and his security.

"Do you consider this a failure or a success?" he asked her, throwing open the door to his office and moving over to stand behind his desk.

"It depends on how you—"

"A success for you, I suppose," interrupted Williams sharply. "And a failure for me."

"You could say that," Ana agreed. She remained standing and speaking in a similar tone to stay on a level field with him. "This event has proven that yes, the patient is being harmed by Passers, but that your Bird Cage is completely ineffective. It's still good for us, though."

"How do you figure?" demanded Williams. "If an electromagnetic field as strong as the Bird Cage can't keep out Passers, there's no way on earth we can protect our guy."

The perplexed look on deTarlo's face confirmed that she had not been thinking anything of the sort.

"This would indeed be a waste of time if he died early on," she muttered softly.

Chester stopped shuffling through the information on his cluttered desk and looked up in disgust.

"Wait outside," he told his security and assistant. His voice was trembling with rage that he managed to hold in until the door was closed.

"You are unbelievable!" Williams exclaimed. "And I mean literally, more so than the presence of buddy-buddy ghosts."

"Chet, calm down," Ana answered, raising her own voice authoritatively. "Don't forget the objective of this project. It was clearly for the purpose of verifying the patient's claims of harassment. Your Bird Cage was simply chosen because it was a controlled environment built for the express purpose of studying Passer activities."

"Well throw a party; you got your answer, didn't you?"

"It was fortunate the thermal imaging cameras actually caught footage of the Passers since they chose to be invisible on the video. I've never seen that on thermal before. Very interesting."

"*I* saw them," Williams replied. "Rod was there, and Kara, even our own Case 2, Cliff Watts. It's very *interesting* alright; an apparent sentinel event."

"What do you mean?"

"Look at your own file," Chester said, snatching the folder from his desk to toss it at her. "Your patient claimed that Watts warned him that he would inherit the Passers of all the former cases, and it seems he has. He was not being attacked by our Passers or by Watts, and now he is. You could conceivably argue it's the hospital's fault."

"That is ridiculous!" deTarlo replied angrily, glancing down at the information in her hands. "The patient was already considered a sentinel event case when he was brought back from a suicide effort. He was released from the hospital only days before he made the attempt on his own life. It was being investigated."

"Well it sounds like you have the whole FBI on this *one* case," Williams stated scornfully. "I don't want to nitpick about details. We don't have the time."

"The patient is stable."

"He's not staying here," Chester informed her, finally sitting down in his chair. "The only way to keep ahead of the Passers seems to be moving him from place to place."

"He claims to be attacked when he travels."

"Listen, Ana," Chester said wearily. "I am not running a private Passer defense organization here. Rod and the other Passers were not themselves around him, and now that they know that, how much control do you think I'll have?"

"You never *had* control," deTarlo replied stingingly, still standing. "You have had to call in a few favors, alright, but where real people are concerned, *you* have done very *little*."

Chester fixed his muddy-ice eyes on her face while he kept his temper in check. He wanted very much to list all the ways he would have made it to where he was now on his own if she had not interfered in his life when he was younger. They'd had the argument repeatedly, yet every time he had conceded to her demands and done some inconvenient favor for her.

But he was gifted long before he met her. He was only months old when the Sentience Awakening began, and many a time, older opponents had claimed he wasn't around to see the beginning.

"How old must one be to witness history?" he'd often said. "I *was* around when the first of the Passers stepped from the shadows to form an unbreakable bond with mankind. It is my goal to strengthen that bond."

"How inspiring," deTarlo had said with a false smile, years ago after his first of many public speeches as she embraced him to passive aggressively claim his success as her own. He could still vividly recall the near-genuine conviction in her eyes.

"Do not speak only of what you *will* do," she had advised sagely, "but also of what you *can* do. You are one of the few who can always see them."

It was true. Chester was one of the few people in the world who could see all Passers at all times. Even when they did not wish to be seen, he could pick up the faint silhouette or shadow of mist that betrayed their presence. It was not always a good thing. Seeing ghosts at all hours had a way of ruining private conversations and intimate situations.

Williams and deTarlo looked to the door as Rod and the ghost of the golden-haired young woman stepped through and stood by quietly. Rod briefly clasped the forearm of the other Passer as if to offer moral support.

"I asked you to stay away," Chester muttered. Rod appeared apologetic and fidgeted with what appeared to be a loosened tie around its neck.

"We're drawn here," it said. "It's like that annoying ache in the back of your brain when you desperately want something, but you don't know what."

DeTarlo's Passer nodded its appealing young face, wearing the same expression of regret. It shifted self-consciously from one bare foot to the other.

Williams angrily thumped his elbow on his desk and rested his head in his hand.

"Get out," deTarlo spoke for him. Both of the spirits looked to her face as if they didn't believe her.

"Kara," the shrink said slowly. "I've seen nothing of you for days. Get out; we'll speak later."

The psychologist's Passer looked resistant, and had the option of refusing to leave, but elected to obey. Rod waited for a few moments to see if Chester would speak before it too departed.

"Your patient isn't staying here," Williams stated again, firmly. "It's your fault he's our responsibility, and now it's going to cost us a fortune to figure out what to do with him."

"Why can't we simply release him?" Ana asked. "Let him fend for himself?"

"Then how would you publish your paper? Finish it with, 'Subject was released and killed on the street out front by the waiting Passers'?"

The doctor's face didn't betray any thoughts as she gazed at him over her glasses. He shuffled through his paperwork until he came out with what he was looking for.

"This," he said, tossing a packet toward her, "is a 'dead zone' in Iowa. It's supposed to be an area where Passers have never been seen, even when traveling with people who go there. They go out of their way to pass *around* it. We've haven't tested it enough to be sure that it's airtight."

"Iowa?" repeated deTarlo. "That's over eight hundred miles away."

"Let's hear your better idea."

"I think we should continue the study."

"Until what? The Passers kill him?"

DeTarlo shrugged and put the file and papers back on his desk. Without speaking to her, Williams picked up the phone and pressed a button.

"Transport office and hold," he said, putting the receiver back in its cradle and rising to his feet.

"Leave my office," he ordered Dr. deTarlo. "This case is no longer a study of psychiatric health. Push me the wrong way, and I'll kick you out of this entirely. It's not going to be another *Study of the Psychological Limits of Vasovagel Syncope.*"

"You don't have the authority to kick me out," Ana replied calmly, turning toward the door. "The patient signed my consent forms too, not yours only."

Williams ignored her and put his phone to his ear.

CHAPTER 6

Aidriel began to float toward the edge of consciousness to the sound of the steady drone of an engine. He was vaguely aware of constant vibration, and could hear and sense people around him.

"Type AB positive," a man was saying.

"Universal recipient," commented a woman. "Probably saved his life a couple of times."

He could hear the watery sound of a bag of liquid being handled. Someone was sniffing and sighing.

"Why are you crying?" asked the man.

"It's just, he's about the same age as my son," another woman replied, "and seeing him like this, oh, you know. I wouldn't want to see my own son like this. It must be horrible for him."

"I wouldn't get too attached to him," replied the first woman. "*I* heard what happened. With stuff like that, I doubt he's going to survive long."

Aidriel wanted to tell her that he agreed with her.

"He's waking up." Dreamer shushed them. "He'll hear you."

Aidriel managed to get his eyes to open and found four faces looking down at him. Dreamer and the first of the other women, a nurse, had long enough hair that it hung around their faces and was moving steadily. They were all riding in the back of some sort of private ambulance.

"Are you in any pain?" asked the man, a doctor. Aidriel attempted to lift his hand to touch his face, but it was strapped down.

"Don't try to move," the second nurse told him. "You've got severe bruising."

"You don't have to tell *me* that," he mumbled miserably.

"And you look like you got mauled," piped in the sniffling nurse, "by a bear."

The other nurse and doctor gave her a dirty look, but she shrugged it off, muttering, "Well, he *does!*"

"How did you *ever* become a nurse?" asked the other nameless woman.

"I worked at a doctor's office; not too often you saw severe injuries or death there. Give me a break, will ya?"

Dreamer's eyes glazed over at the mention of the bear, and she stared listlessly out the side window until Aidriel spoke again.

"Where're we going?" he asked gruffly.

"You're being transported," answered the doctor. "North, toward Lake Erie. I guess the jet couldn't meet us any closer. I don't know how much we're at liberty to tell you, but it was decided the Bird Cage wasn't safe enough."

"Where *is* safe enough?"

"We can't tell you."

"I can't even know where I'm going?"

"No. Are you in any pain?"

"What kind of a question is that?"

The doctor nodded and began to fumble around with something out of Aidriel's line of view, muttering about giving him more analgesic.

Dreamer, who was sitting above Aidriel's head, leaned over him and whispered, "What saved you?"

Aidriel felt a blanketing of calmness and comfort originating from the arm where the shot of painkiller had been administered.

"I don't know," he murmured, blinking heavily. "Ask Williams. He was there."

"*He* won't tell us anything."

"And two orderlies were dismissed," added the sentimental nurse.

"We're just the peons," confirmed the other nurse.

Aidriel moaned and relaxed, sighing in agreement.

Tammy the nurse was leaning against one of the many corners at the hospital in Fort Wayne, a cigarette dangling from her fingertips. She was on break, the day was fine, and she liked this secluded corner under the trees. Birds were singing, but Tammy was paying no attention. If she looked closely, she could see the heads of the men working on the roof of one of the hospital's many wings, and watched as they tossed their refuse into a dumpster below.

Someone very close-by said her name; she jumped and nearly dropped her cigarette. Whirling around, Tammy saw a middle-aged man in a wheelchair, his hands on his lap and his eyes fixed intently on her.

"Oh, Dr. St. Cross!" she said with a sigh of relief. "You startled me."

"Is Matilda keeping you company?" he asked, meaning her Passer.

"She's around somewhere. But how have you been? Did you come for a follow-up?"

"I came to talk to you and a few of your colleagues."

"Oh, okay…"

St. Cross was a slight, restless man, and he flexed his shoulders and clasped his hands in front of his chest before he continued.

"I received a disturbing phone call about Aidriel Akimos."

"He's not here anymore; he was transferred from the psych ward over a week ago."

"Where did he go?"

"Out of state. I thought you knew about it."

St. Cross had not, as deTarlo claimed, retired from his work and was finding it difficult to take it easy outside the loop while he was on medical leave. He sat very still and watched Tammy's face, his keen eyes conveying his wariness to let on that he was in the dark. The nurse took a nervous drag on her cigarette and shifted back and forth on her feet.

"Dr. deTarlo got *A.S.M.* to fly him away somewhere. It was all top secret."

St. Cross's eyes widened minutely with anger and he looked away in thought. He unclasped his hands and flexed the fingers slightly, a sign he was about to become animated.

"Forget for a second about patient confidentiality," he said, "because I believe there is something going on I am unaware of, and my patient is in danger."

Tammy dropped her smoke and stamped it out on the sidewalk, making herself more comfortable against the brick corner.

"I'm very sorry," she apologized, and he made as if to try and convince her, but she quickly continued, "I thought for sure you would be kept up to date. You've been working with Aidriel for years."

"Five," St. Cross agreed.

Tammy looked sympathetic.

"Did anyone tell you he tried to kill himself?" she asked softly. St. Cross's face at once expressed his pain at the news, but not surprise.

"Tried to hang himself a couple weeks ago," explained Tammy.

"And deTarlo finally got Williams' attention."

"Yeah, guess so."

"Well I'll be…," St. Cross mused. "I couldn't get more than a perfunctory letter and she gets Aidriel shipped off to Kelly Road."

"Where?"

St. Cross deliberately changed direction, both literally and figuratively.

"When last I saw him, the attacks were getting worse, and now there's no doubt in my mind that the Passers are to blame."

"You're kidding!" Tammy's mouth hung open for several seconds as she let it sink in. "I just thought he was delusional."

"Unfortunately, that's what everyone seemed to think." St. Cross raised his eyebrows and smacked his lips at the beginning of his sentences, a vaguely annoying habit he fell into when he was trying to make a point. "For the last year and a half it has been my opinion that Aidriel's claims were at least partially true. I tried to garner any information I could from Passerists not only as to the how, but the why. There had to be a good reason why Aidriel was one of a handful of people on the planet who are actually harmed by the spirits."

"And…?"

"I was cleaning the gutters and my ladder fell over, so here I am." He indicated the wheelchair. "My patient was snatched away from me and even from himself."

"What do you mean?"

"I mean the Passers have even more influence than we give them credit for. I think I was not intended to be involved, and now that I'm out of the way, deTarlo and Williams can do whatever they want with Aidriel and my hands are tied."

"Did you ask Andrei about it?"

"Yes, I did. Just before it pushed over the ladder so that I would land on the curb and break my back."

Tammy stared at him as if she didn't believe his Passer was capable of that.

"There's something about Aidriel," said St. Cross, "that makes the Passers forget their good intentions. Andrei has spoken of the Paradox of Natural Judgment."

"Matilda's said something about that too!"

"How the souls of the tortured are the protectors, while those that lived in opulence at the expense of others become tormentors."

"What does that have to do with Aidriel?"

"My theory," said St. Cross, "is that these harmful Passers do not realize they are following a preordained plan. That plan is to kill Aidriel so that as a Passer, he can do some incredibly vital act of aid... Real aid..."

The psychiatrist smiled at his private joke. Tammy was too preoccupied with her own thoughts to notice, and hesitantly asked, "Am I callous to think that doesn't sound so bad?"

St. Cross abruptly changed the subject again: "I actually came here to ask you a pointed question. I've heard recently about dreams that the hospital medical staffers have been having while caring for Aidriel. They all dreamt that they were Passers present at his death, and when his spirit left his body, they attacked and devoured it."

Tammy's face paled and she was struck speechless.

"It appears you too have had the dream," commented the psychiatrist. "As have I. As has anyone I have specifically asked, and can confirm that it is indeed Aidriel. Perhaps everyone at one time in their life has had it...."

"What do you think it means?"

"It means Aidriel's going to die."

Before leaving for the dead zone, deTarlo had taken the time to rebuke Kara, but Williams was too busy to bother with his own Passer. Just before leaving, he'd tried to find the ghost to no avail, and surmised it had left the area.

Chester had actually known of Rod indirectly before the Passer's death. Rod's life ended when Chester was a boy, through tragic circumstances. Though Chester had never seen Rod in living form, the Passerist knew Rod's brother, Craig.

Craig had the misfortune of being attracted to a young woman who resided across the street from the apartment building on Balete Drive where Chester had lived with his father when he was a child. On the second date with the girl, Craig was walking her to her door in the new-moon darkness after a late dinner. The young lady's vindictive ex-boyfriend or ex-husband—Chester couldn't remember which—was waiting in the shadows, and attacked with the intent of killing the woman he considered his own. Craig intervened, and for his efforts, received a bullet to the head at point-blank range. He didn't die immediately. Craig was conscious for eight minutes, bleeding to death on the sidewalk while the ambulance rushed unsuccessfully to save him.

The noise of the struggle, the shot, and the girl's screams drew the attention of several of the neighbors, including Chester. Awakening and crawling out of bed and to his window, the then-young Passerist saw lights coming on in casements up and down the street. The attacker saw the activity too, and fled the scene, but was later caught by the police. Chester had opened his pane, and the night was quiet enough for him to hear the young woman's frantic sobs and Craig's pathetic, garbled effort at last words. One does not forget witnessing such a thing, even from a distance.

The girl involved moved away shortly after the murder and was never heard from again. Strongly affected by the horror of his death, Craig's Passer wandered the streets for years, becoming a homeless resident. It was possible it had not been assigned a living companion by whomever it was that arranged such things. Chester was on speaking

90

terms with it. He could recall even as a boy feeling that it was a shame Craig had died; the Passer had a good sense of humor. Williams and many of the neighbors were saddened by Craig's final release to pass on when the killer was executed.

Rod was close with his brother when both of them were alive, and was absolutely devastated by Craig's death. Overwhelmed with grief, Rod spent days numbing the pain with alcohol. Only days after the murder, Rod walked down to the beach at nightfall to guzzle Everclear and mourn, and passed out drunk on the sand. The tide came in, and Rod went out. Chester sent the unfortunate mother a card of condolence at the loss of both of her sons within a week. He never knew what became of her and had wondered all the years since. The Passers of her children didn't know or wouldn't say.

Rod did not immediately become Chester's Passer companion. Williams grew up in the company of first a preteen boy, then a middle-aged man, both of whom were closer to Chester than any living relationships. Each parting was painful, but Williams knew it was inevitable that the Passers would eventually be released from their purgatory to, as the name Passersby indicated, pass on to oblivion.

When Rod came to Chester, Williams was in his mid-twenties, a difficult time in his life. His relationship with his parents was rocky and the choices he was procrastinating to make for his future were unclear. Rod, despite his untimely demise, was an anchor; a perfect example, it turned out, of why Passers were so priceless in the lives of those still confined to flesh and blood. While still alive, Rod was a poet or a teacher or the like,

91

whose life was well in order for being in his mid-thirties. While a spirit, Rod was instrumental in helping Chester find a solid psychological foundation.

Though he'd never be so insensitive as to voice it, Williams secretly felt that he had somehow taken Craig's place for Rod, and that the Passer needed him to be as close as a brother. Of course the ghosts still had emotions; they were bodiless souls, not just wise holograms as so many critics tried to portray them. Chester understood them—he had spent years shirking living company for the Passers that never made themselves seen; those were the most fragile. The ones that carried the most pain, suffered the most grief, and hid themselves to keep it muted and private.

But Chester could always see them; he could corner and drag the secrets out of any of them. He began to recognize the signs of pain that the Passers displayed, and could perceive it in the people he knew, who were even more careful than the dead to hide it. Pain was all around, but though personalized, it was all the same.

"Do you agree with her at all?" Rod had asked him after deTarlo made the comment about Passers becoming unneeded in their first meeting about Aidriel.

"No, not in the slightest," Chester responded with all certainty. "We need each other, your kind and mine. We save each other."

Rod was clearly troubled, but nodded. "I save others by atonement," it said. "The horror that happened to me can be prevented from happening to others."

"Is that how you'll achieve the peace to pass on?" Chester asked, dreading the answer.

"Not for *many* years, my friend," Rod assured him. "I can tell you with all certainty that I will stand by you until the day you die."

Williams's dismay at the subject evaporated instantly.

"Good," he said. "Now let's figure out the problem at hand. This man that claims the Passers harm him."

"You'll have things to learn from this man," foretold Rod. "But in the meantime, I will tell you something about the near future. In Iowa, when they become aggressive, you'll have to walk away. You won't want to, but you've got to remember I warned you to walk away, and you have to do it immediately."

"Iowa? When am I going to be there? And who are *they*?"

"You'll know when the time comes. You have to trust me. Do you?"

"I always have."

"Alright. Now we can focus on Kelly Road."

The ambulance hit some kind of rough patch in the road and jostled harshly. At least that was what the nurses told Aidriel when he awoke with a start.

"You're fine, just a bump," the sentimental one said.

"Felt like we hit something," he mumbled. He must have been out for hours, because the painkiller had worn off.

93

"Nope," they all said at once, except Dreamer, who was looking over her shoulder and out the windshield of the van.

Aidriel lay still and listened, his ears straining to catch any threatening sounds through the clearing fog imposed on his brain by too much sleep. The ambulance bounced and jolted again, and the driver muttered a curse. The medical mercenaries all sat in silent tension.

"Unstrap me," Aidriel said. "I can't protect my head when I'm like this."

"You can't protect your head anyway," said the doctor without thinking.

The engine promptly sputtered and died, and the driver began to cuss more vehemently. The passengers could hear honking horns outside the vehicle and it began to wobble and violently shake. The doctor and nurses scrambled to hold onto something.

Aidriel felt pain in the pit of his stomach, and his ears began to ring. He was defenseless, not to mention drained and still recovering from his last encounter.

The ambulance continued to shake powerfully, the driver panicking and cursing, turning the wheel with all his strength.

"I can't brake!" he yelled out. "I can't steer!"

Afraid to speak, the travelers braced themselves, the rapid breathing of the women coming out in soft, frightened gasps. It sounded as if the vehicle went onto a shoulder, scraping against a metal guardrail. The doctor was beginning to shout something to the driver when a great force struck the side of the van nearest Aidriel. The ambulance tilted dangerously, then crashed back down on all its wheels.

Aidriel turned his head up to look for Dreamer and saw her tense face.

"Unstrap my arms!" he called to her, and without hesitation, she reached over him to comply. He got a glimpse of her hands, the knuckles still white from clutching the side of the stretcher. The instant his arms were free, he sat up and undid the other strap across his legs. Another blow against the side of the ambulance set it harshly rocking and Aidriel slid off the stretcher into the knees of the doctor and nurses, who held onto one another in terror. Dreamer lost her balance and ended up bent over the stretcher, gripping the sides of the secured cot for support.

As soon as the vehicle had dropped to its wheels again, Aidriel balanced himself on his feet and reached around Dreamer to find a secure grip, squeezing his fingers into the gap on the other side of the gurney just before the next blow. Once more, the ambulance ground against the guardrail, teetering perilously up on two wheels and finally tumbling over. Aidriel clutched the sides of the stretcher with one arm over Dreamer to shield her, and bent his legs around the framework of the cot as they fell.

Everyone screamed when the van tipped over the rail and tumbled down a high embankment. It rolled several times and flailing bodies struck against one another and the inside of the vehicle. Aidriel managed to hang on to the stretcher, but one of the medical workers fell hard against his back as they rolled, driving his abdomen into the table with enough force to knock the breath clean out of him.

A foot hit his shoulder; a knee found the side of his head. Dreamer was turned away. Aidriel couldn't see her face and didn't hear her screaming. He wondered if she would slip out from under him.

For several breathless seconds the ambulance spun down to the bottom of the ditch. It came to a smashed rest on its right side, the travelers inside lying in aching tangles.

Aidriel lost his grip and tipped backward, his legs still hooked around the stretcher. The back of his head smashed into one of the overhead storage cupboards. Instantly dizzy, he couldn't tell who it was that took him by the arms and dragged him out the back door of the wrecked vehicle. It hurt to have his lower limbs so roughly jerked from the metal framework inside, and he was instantly flooded with panic to think that the Passers were taking him away. He tried to struggle, but resistance was entirely out of his control.

Suddenly finding himself unceremoniously dropped into the grass and left to lie there, Aidriel stared up at the trees and power lines running alongside the road. He heard voices, and realized there were no internal warning signs. Turning his head painfully, he felt a stinging sensation on the back of his scalp. The doctor was sitting next to him, tending an injured arm, but appearing rather lucid. The sentimental nurse was pacing, sobbing, ignoring the pleading of an orderly to sit down and take it easy. An orderly? There were none in the ambulance, how had they reached the crash so quickly? Had he lost time?

Dreamer was sitting several yards away on the side of the embankment, her knees drawn up to her chest and her head in her hands. DeTarlo was bending over her, her voice raised and her arms jerking wildly as she poked at the phleb and pointed out at nothing.

Aidriel sat up and mimicked Dreamer's head cradling. The pain was incredible. The doctor was talking to him, but words weren't registering. The crying nurse was shaking her head and repeating that she couldn't "do it anymore."

DeTarlo approached and leaned over to look at him. She too asked him questions he couldn't make any sense of. She was very agitated, going so far as to touch his head and tilt his face up so she could see it. The shrink gave the doctor an order and he got stiffly to his feet. In a few moments, he returned with some medical supplies. They each took one of Aidriel's shoulders, pushing him back so he was lying down again. He felt the poke of a needle in his arm, and the pain faded away.

Before the analgesic kicked in, Dreamer was so battered and sore, she could hardly stand it. Sitting on the side of the hill, involuntary tears streaming down her cheeks, she pitied herself and wondered what in the world she was doing here. She didn't even know what limb to cradle because all of them ached so acutely.

Most of the other members of Williams's entourage were already gone, shuttled off in small groups to who knew where. Aidriel was one of the first to go, so the Passers in the area were waiting around calmly, as if they too would have a turn to be transported.

Dreamer's Passer, Tracy, sat down beside the girl and watched her with a meek expression.

"What is the matter with all of you?" Dreamer asked miserably. "Why do you do it?"

"I don't know," Tracy said softly. It looked over the wreckage and made a sound like a sigh, stroking the front of its wool coat in a habitual effort to smooth it.

Dreamer wiped her nose with the back of her hand and saw a streak of blood on her skin. She was used to seeing the red liquid contained in tidy vials or in little droplets on gauze. It was darker in the airtight tubes; a rich crimson. Dreamer didn't like the color of blood on her skin, bright like a streak of paint.

She was used to dreams about blood. It usually appeared as a passive ingredient in the collage of her nighttime visions. But it had been different of late. She'd had recurring dreams where she was standing in the middle of the street, hosing away a large bloodstain in the middle of the asphalt. Tracy didn't know what it meant; no one that Dreamer had casually asked about it seemed to be able to shed any light on the mystery.

Tracy turned its head slowly back and forth, scanning its surroundings indifferently.

"What are you thinking about?" asked Dreamer, glancing at her watch and wondering how much longer it would be until the painkiller kicked in.

"The future," responded the ghost. "And the past."

"Anything but the present, huh?" Dreamer tried to smile through her grimace.

"Do you think about what you're experiencing at the moment?" questioned Tracy.

"If it merits thought, yeah. Why're we having a philosophical conversation now?"

"I supposed that perhaps I should distract you."

"Not working."

"I'm sorry. Will you stay on?"

"You mean with Williams? I didn't think I had a choice at this point."

"You do. No one can force you to do anything."

Dreamer gritted her teeth in pain as he stretched out her legs one at a time to get the blood flowing in them.

"I know that," she said. Tracy had been telling her similar things her whole life.

"Make up your mind, then," Tracy stated. "Stick to it and defend it."

"You mean never admit to making a mistake, even when you do?" Dreamer was skeptical.

"I mean no one can tell you what is right. When you decide something for yourself, you don't have to back down unless *you* want to."

"I'll keep that in mind." Dreamer didn't bother to hide her sarcasm. She was too uncomfortable to appreciate that Tracy was waxing poetic.

"So will you stay?" Tracy asked.

"Yeah." Dreamer was not in the mood for chitchat.

"For the job or for the man?"

"Williams?"

"No, Aidriel."

Dreamer looked at Tracy's young, unassuming face. They'd been close Dreamer's whole life, and had told each other everything. Growing up, Dreamer looked to the ageless Tracy for guidance for girl troubles, both physical and emotional. The spirit had been protector, mother, sister and friend, and though barely adequate in the roles, Tracy had been better than no one at all. But considering how the Passers acted in regard to Aidriel, Dreamer was disinclined to say much about a certain growing attraction.

"It's a puzzle," she lamely explained. "I'd like to know what's going on. I don't suppose you can offer any insight?"

Tracy made a face at Dreamer's first statement like it didn't believe her, then shook its head at her question.

"Were you involved in that attack in the Bird Cage?" asked Dreamer.

"No," Tracy said instantly.

"And the ambulance?"

"No, I had nothing to do with it."

"So you haven't been around at any of the attacks?"

"No, but I am aware of them."

It didn't occur to Dreamer that Tracy might lie to her.

"But you don't know why they're happening?" she wanted to know.

"No. I *don't* know why."

Dreamer knew Tracy well enough to pick up on the fact that the Passer didn't want to discuss the subject further. Perhaps the ghost itself was upset by the attacks, or knew something bad about other Passers that it would prefer not to reveal.

"Okay, so I guess I'll just stay outside the loop," Dreamer muttered, more to herself than to Tracy. The Passer was unmoved by the comment, and watched one of Williams's cars return to pick up the last of the lingering employees.

The painkiller was finally beginning to kick in, and Dreamer stood up, relieved to find the aches in her limbs slowly easing.

"You can't come with me," she told Tracy.

"It's alright," agreed the Passer. "Another destination demands my presence."

Dreamer walked away and didn't hear Tracy add, "We're both going west. I will see you there."

CHAPTER 7

Dr. St. Cross sat in his home office wearing a phone headset and numbly shifting his wheelchair back and forth by the wheels. His jade eyes were fixed on the large glass aquarium across the room, in which several brightly colored snakes slid noiselessly over a tangle of branches. The music coming through the headset was painfully monotonous, but he patiently waited.

"American Sentience Movement, how may I help you?" a voice said finally.

"Intern Jack Stickney, please," the shrink requested.

"Hold please."

The music resumed briefly, then the line clicked, and Stickney answered.

The psychiatrist spoke briskly: "Jack, it's Dr. St. Cross from Saint Michael Hospital."

"Oh. Hello, Doc." The intern on the line sounded less than thrilled.

"I wonder if you could tell me where Chester Williams is. I can't seem to contact him; he's out of town, I'm told."

"Yes, he's out of town. He will check his messages when he gets back."

"You couldn't just tell me where he is?"

"Why in the world would I do that?"

"C'mon Jack, you know why I'm calling. I can't seem to get in touch with Dr. deTarlo either, and it's urgent."

"It would have to be *extremely* urgent."

"Oh it is. It's in regards to their patient."

"Their patient." If Jack knew what St. Cross was talking about, he was doing a good job of sounding clueless.

"Look, it's no secret that Kelly Road got a green light. I just need to talk with deTarlo or Chester as soon as possible."

Jack sighed a long, heavy sigh. He sounded very put out, but he always did. St. Cross had been in contact with this particular intern several times over the last year in his mission to bring Aidriel to the attention of the organization's lead Passerist. Finally, Jack had given in and written a report about the case, which he sent to Williams, who had read and dismissed it. Ever since, Stickney didn't bother to hide his annoyance when the psychiatrist continued to call him.

St. Cross could hear Jack tapping his keyboard and making soft affirmations to himself while he looked for information. It surprised the shrink that the intern didn't know immediately where Kelly Road was located.

"How's your internship going, by the way?" St. Cross asked in a friendly tone.

"Could be better."

"Oh, I apologize, but my offer to show you around the Psychology Center will have to be postponed indefinitely."

"Oh?"

"I had an accident and find myself confined to a chair on wheels."

"A car accident?"

"No."

"You couldn't reach anyone at Kelly Road 'cause they aren't there anymore."

St. Cross was simultaneously surprised and concerned.

"Where are they?"

"The most current status says they're in Ohio, traveling northwest by car. The itinerary appears to be to meet the jet in Cleveland."

"They're on the move, then."

"Yes."

"Is there any way to get a message to them?"

"If it's a *very* urgent message, I can have it sent to Williams's personal cell, though he won't like it if it's not important."

"It *is* important."

"Go ahead."

"Tell him St. Cross wants his patient back."

Jack hung up on him. In an uncharacteristic display of anger, the psychiatrist flung away his headset and slammed his fist down on his desk.

Chester and deTarlo's yelling match awakened Aidriel from a sound sleep, and he found himself in a bed at a fancy hotel; the name *The Pen Ryn* was embroidered above the silhouette of a White House–esque building emblazoned on the decorative pillows around his head. He ached all over, but his first thought was how strange it was that he was quite used to awakening in foreign places. It was usually a hospital, though, which was very unlike a suite like this.

The Passerist and the psychologist were standing on either side of the little dining table by the kitchenette, apparently oblivious to the effect they were having on anyone else in the room.

"I'm putting my license on the line," deTarlo snapped. "It was impossibly difficult to keep local rescue from getting involved."

"It's a moot point," replied Williams, visibly harried. "No one wants to go any further. I'm not prepared to offer them the money they'd require to stay on."

"Then you think we should cut our losses and leave."

Chester paused with his mouth open, his brow bent in a thoughtful frown. He ran a hand through the back of his short blond hair, the knuckles of the other resting in a fist against the tabletop.

"Look," Ana began, her voice softened to try and convince him. "I've thought of this possibility, and the best thing we can do is *press on*. We can't just cut the whole thing loose."

"Whole *thing*?" Chester retorted. "This is a dangerous mess that is spiraling out of control."

"What would you suggest we do? We *have* to keep going."

"Do you want to drive him, then? No one else does!"

"I said I would," cut in Dreamer, who was lying on the couch in the sitting area, her elbow bent over her face to shield her eyes. The television was on at a low volume, the channel set at some sensational biography show about a garage band that had been struck by lightning during an outdoor concert.

"Oh yeah, *you* will." Ana laughed aloud, and Dreamer moved her arm to give the psychologist a dirty look.

"If she wants to, let her," Williams said dismissively. "No one else will. Literally everyone we specifically hired for this has hightailed it for the hills, and with good reason."

"Everyone but me," pointed out deTarlo.

"Do I suddenly not exist?" asked Dreamer, getting up to approach them. "I said *I* would drive him. If I have to, I'll rent my own car and pay for my own gas. We've come this far; *I'll* go all the way."

The shrink shook her head so vehemently, her usually flawless updo flopped loose. Williams arched his eyebrow at them both.

"What are you again?" he asked Dreamer.

"Besides a person? A phlebotomist."

"Right. I don't have a clue why he was so insistent you come along, but we appeased him. Doesn't make you irreplaceable or anything."

Dreamer narrowed her eyes but didn't take the bait to start a personal argument.

"What is the big deal here, anyway?" she asked. "I said I'd drive him, and neither of you are willing to take a chance for someone else. Just throw money at it, maybe it'll go away. I'm actually kind of surprised you even came along to see him off."

In one swift movement, Chester stepped toward her and slapped her across the face.

"Watch your attitude, you snide little!—"

Aidriel collided with Chester with enough force to drive the latter into the table.

"Screw you and your self-righteous club," Aidriel spat.

Dreamer did not react to the blow besides lowering her blazing eyes. She was used to taking such harsh treatment without responding emotionally; hitting had been the favorite anger outlet for a former guardian of hers, and he had not been tolerant of reciprocation of any sort.

"Knock it off!" ordered deTarlo, hushing them all. "I am still in charge here; listen to me. Dreamer will drive Aidriel to the 'dead zone,' and Chet and I will follow behind in a separate vehicle."

"What 'dead zone'?" Aidriel asked crossly, massaging his aching right shoulder.

"There is a place in Iowa that is thought to be a natural dead area to Passers," Ana explained impatiently. "That's where we were taking you."

Aidriel grimaced and felt the tender bruise on the back of his head.

"Why am I being taken anywhere?" he demanded. "Why don't we just go home to Fort Wayne?"

DeTarlo smiled slightly.

"Maybe you should read consent forms before you sign them," she retorted snarkily. "You agreed in writing to be dependent upon our judgment until the completion of our study."

"I thought the study was over."

"The study isn't over until a substantiated conclusion can be drawn in reference to your claims that the Passers are attacking you."

"You already had your proof."

"There weren't any Passers at the ambulance crash when we got there."

"You got your proof in the Bird Cage."

108

"I would be willing to show you my table and hypothesis if you insist," the shrink answered patronizingly. "It clearly outlines required conclusions necessary to publish this study, including the cause behind the attacks."

"Ask the Passers, then," Dreamer cut in, having recovered from the shock of the slap. "Don't you think if he knew the cause, we wouldn't be here?"

"What the hell do you think I've been spending my time doing?" snapped Chester. "I don't know if you noticed, girl, but the Passers have been noticeably MIA from the start of this whole thing, except for, of course, when they're mucking things up."

Dreamer flashed a disappointed half-smile but didn't reply.

Aidriel sat down on the arm of one of the two easy chairs in the room to rest his aching legs. He was manifestly weary and sighed silently, his gaze drifting to the floor in thought. His hand moved involuntarily up to feel his throat, where the injuries caused by his attempt to end his life had faded away. As his fingers closed slightly around his neck, he recalled vividly the sensation of the rope tightening. It had burned his skin and lungs, but the blackness was beautiful. Suffocation was a miserable way to go, and he had felt it both before and since the hanging.

But there was something liberating about dangling like that, being washed out into the sea of death, suspended, instead of curled up on the floor. When he had lost his sight before blacking out entirely, Aidriel had felt as if he were a part of the sky, floating free. There was nothing and no one around to press in and imprison him, only a total lack of boundaries, like the swirling of the winds. He hated being smothered, and that was how he was feeling now.

The urge to run returned, like when he had sensed the Passers converging on the Bird Cage. These people were just as bloodthirsty and unreasonable as the spirits. And he had signed his freedom away without considering how much worse it was than being on his own. It suddenly dawned on him, however, that he was not entirely helpless; he needed only to sign something else.

The others had waited with patient curiosity while Aidriel mused, and they looked on expectantly when he once more found his feet.

"Dr. deTarlo, could I speak with you in private?" he asked, his voice calm and soft. Dreamer and Chester exchanged a surprised look but did not comment.

"We'll see about a car," stated Williams. Dreamer pursed her lips in disappointment, but reluctantly followed the Passerist out of the room, the red shape of his handprint still visible on her cheek.

Williams's security staff and assistant were set up in an adjoining suite, waiting at his beck and call. Chester paused in the open doorway, thoughtfully regarding the men at their busy work.

"Nearest car rental," he requested of his slim assistant, who typed and clicked hurriedly on his laptop for a minute or two before telling Williams the address.

"Would you like for me to set up a rental?" the assistant asked, his hand hovering at the ready over his mouse.

"It's within walking distance, yes? I'll go there myself. I need to get out of here for a while."

"Just six blocks, on Annie's Street." The assistant quickly entered the address into a GPS device and handed it over to Chester. For several moments, the Passerist examined the map and route on the touch screen without speaking. Dreamer noticed one of the security staff was peering outside through binoculars from behind the moleskin curtains on the farthest of the windows, reminding her of a spy flick.

"Alright," Chester said when he was satisfied with the information he had gleaned. He gathered a few things from a table near the door. Stepping out, Williams gestured for Dreamer to come. She hesitated, but realized it was within his power to block her from seeing Aidriel, even if she punished the unacceptable way he had treated her by quitting.

In the elevator, they stared silently forward, she caressing her stinging cheek, he pulling a knit cap down over his hair and zipping up his jacket. He looked at her thoughtfully and saw the mark on her face, but did not apologize.

"You'll get a raise," he said nonchalantly, as if that was all required to avoid a lawsuit. "A substantial one. And a car or something."

Dreamer furrowed her brow unhappily, opening her mouth to reply but checking herself. If she had to turn the other cheek to hang on to her part in this, she would. She could be tolerant. They were coming back to her now, the things she'd heard about Chester's famous temper. She'd just have to tread more carefully from now on.

They passed through the lobby and out onto the sidewalk, Williams glancing at the GPS and turning left, slipping sunglasses on simultaneously. Dreamer took a few quick hop-steps to catch up and walk beside him. She winced at the pain in her limbs that the swift movement caused, and wished she had taken more painkillers before they left. The bruising effects of the ambulance crash were still very present to her nerves.

On the outside *The Pen Ryn* looked nothing like the building printed as its logo; it was high and grand and surveyed the surrounding city center with gleaming window eyes, but was only a rectangular skyscraper. It was not the tallest building in the area, but the muted stonework was impressive from the front, nothing like the nondescript cement wall that filled the view from the parking garage at the rear. Looking up and back over her shoulder at it, Dreamer got the awed sense of being little and inexperienced in a major city. While Fort Wayne was not a small town, the phlebotomist had not traveled much, and was largely impressed by her surroundings. She impulsively wanted to express her wide-eyed interest to Williams, but he was clearly unmoved by the sights.

For the first block neither spoke, and they pretended to be oblivious to the presence of the other. Chester looked around continuously, and Dreamer saw that he was looking at the faces of all the spirits nearby. He even looked for seconds at a time at what appeared to her to be nothing at all, though she assumed he could see the invisible spirits. Her Passer was nowhere to be seen.

"What did it look like?" Dreamer asked finally, turning sideways to avoid a woman with a stroller coming in the opposite direction.

"What did *what* look like?" responded Williams, his eyes fixed straight ahead.

"The attack in the Bird Cage."

"It looked like a mob of Passers beating someone to death."

Dreamer wanted more details, but couldn't think of how to ask.

"Why do you think the Passers didn't stick around after the ambulance crashed?" she inquired instead.

"You got me. It's as if they do strange things like that just to throw us, so we don't know what to expect."

Up ahead, Williams's Passer, Rod, appeared from around a corner and stopped to wait on the sidewalk, exchanging nods of greeting with Chester and falling into step beside them.

"My friend," Rod greeted in the manner that Passers used only when speaking to their living companion.

"Where have you been?" asked Williams.

"Wandering." It was what Passers always said when they were asked their whereabouts.

"I can speak plainly about your 'patient' while I am far from him," Rod continued after a moment. "My deepest desire since first I clapped eyes on him has been to harm him. Even now, it requires my strongest resolve not to run to where he is and attack."

"Why's that?" Chester asked calmly. Rod appeared to exhale slowly and shrug, its face grim and resolute. Dreamer watched the Passer tensely, wondering if it would do as it said.

"Something about him inspires the purest, hottest of hatreds," the ghost explained. "All control is lost in the instinct to cause him pain."

Dreamer glared at the Passer, but wasn't noticed.

The spirits were, for all intents and purposes, humans without bodies. While they were often plagued by the pain of their demise, they could also feel other emotions and were influenced by conversation. They could not fly or travel from one place to another any faster than they could run, and she was pretty sure they were not often, if ever, seen in any type of vehicle while it was moving. Their range of vision and knowledge was only as broad as their experiences, but they had an uncanny sense of what would happen next. Because of this sense, they often affected the outcome of future events.

Though she was not old enough to have seen the beginning of the Sentience, Dreamer had learned of it in her history education at school, and had seen videos online and on television. She had witnessed the records of the greatest kindnesses the Passers had done, including showing engineers the flaws in trains and airplanes, warning about impending floods and fires, and even guiding lost travelers out of the wilderness. Everyone had experienced a lifesaving intervention by a Passer at some time in their life. Dreamer's was when she was ten and was on a camping trip with her Girl

Scout troop. She still had nightmares about the bear.

"This trip makes me miss the protests," Chester commented bitterly, breaking a brief silence.

"You'd rather be cussed at and have stuff thrown at you?" Dreamer asked him. Williams shrugged his shoulders but smirked.

"What exactly is the upset now, anyway?" asked the phleb. "I haven't been keeping informed."

"Overpopulation," Chester answered. "People seem to think that Passers are preventing too many deaths, and that the world is becoming overpopulated."

"Is that true?"

"Of course not. Passers prevent such a small amount of accidents, it isn't making much difference. People still die of natural causes and illnesses, suicides have increased, and many accidental deaths are because people are less cautious. They think that because Passers can see what is coming, that they'll prevent *every* death. If there is no warning, people think there must be no danger."

"Doesn't that tie in with why the Passers are here?"

"In what way do you mean?"

"I mean the belief that Passers aren't supposed to be here. The Sentience was an extreme imbalance in the spiritual planes, most likely an accidental one that the Passers took advantage of, and there aren't supposed to be so many of them. Ghosts used to be mostly oblivious to living people, but now they are controlling and try to bend the real

115

world to how they want it. It's unnatural how the dead hold so much sway over the living. The rate or manner in which people are dying is directly affected by the ghosts and is only increasing their number. The Passers are power-hungry."

As she spoke, she glanced distrustfully at Rod, but the spirit did not appear to be listening.

"That's a popular view on things." Chester's tone kept his opinion about her statement ambiguous.

"It's kind of the *only* view that makes sense," Dreamer pointed out. "Aidriel could really be a poster child for it. If the naysayers heard about him, they'd have a perfect example to support their hatred for the Passers and their intrusion."

"That's not going to happen." Williams's voice steeled almost threateningly. "That would be a bad thing for *A.S.M.*"

"How would deTarlo's report about Aidriel affect the protests, then?"

Chester made a face and stuffed his hands in his pockets, hunching his shoulders as he walked.

"That was a part of our contract," he said. "In exchange for using the Bird Cage, she had to sign an agreement that the study would not be published for at least eighteen months."

"And what did you plan to do with Aidriel when the study was completed?"

Williams shrugged.

"To tell you the truth, I was skeptical enough at the beginning that I didn't think it would matter. I thought he was just a head case, and would be locked up when we were finished."

Rod turned suddenly on its heel and faced the direction they had come from, standing still and staring back at the hotel. The look of hatred was visible on its face, but it restrained itself from moving.

"We need to get a move on," Dreamer commented, slowing to glance back.

Williams continued forward without pause, and she painfully quickened her pace to follow.

At the rental shop, Williams had the clerk put the vehicle's rental in Dreamer's name, as he had intended when he told her to come along, though he was the one to plunk down a card to pay for it. The clerk assumed as a result that Chester and Dreamer were a couple and made a comment to that effect, ignoring the resulting awkward glance from the phleb. The Passerist didn't bother to correct him and told Dreamer to sign the agreement.

The new smartphone in Williams's pocket rang several times while they waited at the counter for the card to go through. In irritation, Chester took out the cell and glanced at the display, which read "Olivia."

"I need to take this," he told Dreamer, leaving her to handle the rest of the paperwork while he stepped outside.

Once on the sidewalk, Chester hit the ANSWER button, staring at the pavement.

"It's Liv," the woman on the other end said.

"I know. Are you alright?"

"Yeah, are you? I heard there was an accident."

"I wasn't in the vehicle when it happened."

Olivia exhaled heavily in relief.

"Bonnie broke her finger yesterday; I took her to the hospital."

Chester cursed under his breath, turning to glance through the window of the business. Dreamer appeared lost where the paperwork was concerned and was looking to see if he was done and could come help her.

"What happened?"

"One of her little friends accidentally closed a door on her. She was really upset; cried herself hoarse. She wanted you."

Williams grimaced, resting his hand on the wall and leaning against it.

"I'm sorry about that," he said.

"Don't apologize. I've told you, I love the munchkin."

"Did you have to stay at the hospital long?"

"Yeah, you know ERs. I miss you."

"You always say that when I'm gone."

"I always mean it."

Chester looked up and saw Dreamer was talking to the clerk, who was getting impatient.

"I have to go now, Liv," he said. As he was taking the phone from his ear to hang up, he heard Olivia tell him she loved him, but he'd pressed the END CALL button before he thought to respond.

CHAPTER 8

Dr. St. Cross's Passer, Andrei, stood at the foot of the shrink's bed, wearing what had been a khaki button-up shirt, watching and waiting for the man to awaken. The psychiatrist had been spending a lot of time asleep as of late since he switched to an analgesic that made him drowsy. His doctor kept insisting rest was required for healing, and though he complied, St. Cross didn't voice his doubts that he would recover any faster than he already was.

Blue velvet curtains were drawn over the blinds in the bedroom windows, creating an illusion of night that made Andrei all the clearer in its pale, hazy form. The temperature in the room began to fall and St. Cross shivered in his sleep, slowly coming around when he felt the bed shutter. Andrei was gripping one of the corner knobs on the footboard.

"Wake up, I have something important to tell you," it said.

St. Cross propped his head up on his elbow, blinking repeatedly to clear away the sleep. There was an uneasy truce between the psychiatrist and his Passer after the accident, and though it had been discussed more than once, Andrei could shed little light on what had happened.

"I saw what I would do," it'd explained vaguely, "and I did it."

Even St. Cross's psychiatric mind could not solve the puzzle of Andrei's future sight.

"I have learned," said Andrei now, "that your patient is being taken to the dead zone in Wellsburg, Iowa."

St. Cross looked lost and continued to blink.

"With this knowledge among my kind," continued Andrei, "there will be a much more concerted effort to prevent him from arriving at any safety. If you want to find him alive, you should go immediately to where he is in Ohio."

St. Cross shook his head to become more awake and said, "Go get Todd to help me."

Williams had his staff load plastic tubs of clothing and supplies into the trunks of the rental car and his own vehicle. He, deTarlo, Dreamer and Aidriel sat lined up on the stone wall bordering the raised flower bed behind the hotel, watching. The patient and phleb were both hanging their heads sleepily, their eyes struggling to stay open against a stupor thanks to their pills.

"You need to wake up," deTarlo said to Dreamer. "You're an accident waiting to happen."

Dreamer appeared offended and blinked rapidly, picked up her cardboard coffee cup and took a drink. The caffeine had not seemed to kick in yet.

The trunks being slammed startled Aidriel and he rubbed his right eye with the heel of his hand. He got to his feet to stretch and the others followed suit. Chester's assistant finished programming the

GPS device in the dashboard of the rental and slid out of the driver's seat, leaving the keys in the ignition for Dreamer.

"You're all set," he told her, shuffling through some papers and handing her the ones regarding the rental, along with printed directions and a credit card.

"We're only about an hour and a half from the airport," deTarlo told the phlebotomist. "You can sleep on the plane. You need to stay very alert."

Dreamer pursed her lips and swallowed, nodding. She was becoming more alert as the gravity of the situation sank in.

Aidriel blearily fumbled with the handle on the side of the car, slid into the passenger seat and strapped in. Dreamer walked over to the still-open driver's door, but stopped when deTarlo gripped her sleeve at the elbow.

"Be very careful," the psychologist said, appearing to be concerned. "We all think he's very important."

Dreamer nodded neutrally, pulling her arm away and entering the car. Williams, deTarlo and the others got into the second vehicle, and both engines started at the same time.

As she pulled out onto the highway, Dreamer glanced at the reflection in the rearview mirror of the car following them. The computerized voice of the GPS told her to drive point-eight miles and merge onto a ramp to the expressway.

Aidriel crossed his arms and leaned his head against the window, closing his eyes.

"Turn on the radio," he mumbled.

Dreamer glanced at him and asked, "Why?"

"I don't like the quiet."

She flicked on the stereo and scanned until she found a station she liked, spinning the steering wheel to turn onto the ramp. Aidriel drifted to sleep easily.

When he first awoke, Aidriel felt as if he had been sleeping for only minutes and was a little stiff. He was still awfully lethargic and wasn't entirely aware of what was happening. The radio was quieter than before, and Dreamer was continually glancing into the rearview mirror. She was driving very quickly, weaving back and forth on the expressway around other cars, her eyes ever darting between the road and the mirrors.

For several minutes, this frenetic driving persisted and only then did Aidriel begin to wonder if something was wrong. He didn't feel the usual fear or sense danger. Perhaps Dreamer was just running behind schedule or was lost.

The engine's growl increased as the phleb continued to accelerate, flying around a truck and down a steep hill. Getting as close as possible behind another car, she maneuvered to the left and slipped in front of a semi at the last moment, gunning it to stay ahead before pulling back into the right lane. Clicking on her signal, Dreamer took a tightly curving ramp, riding the brakes to keep control before rolling to a complete stop at a red light. She was still keeping a close eye on her mirrors, and Aidriel noticed she was firmly gripping the wheel with both hands. He looked out the windshield, but didn't recognize the area or the names on the street signs. Unconcerned and still sleepy, he drifted off again.

****

When Aidriel had tried to leave Indiana of his own accord, it had not sunk in until the third attempt how trapped he really was. Twice already he had tried driving out by car and had crashed as a direct result of the Passers' interference. The third time, he spent most of the money he had saved up to buy a sport motorcycle. Surely it would be easier to avoid the ghosts on a smaller vehicle, or so he thought.

He left at a random time, leaping up from the kitchen table as if it was spontaneous, abandoning his canned soup. Perhaps the Passers would be caught off guard. There was only time to grab a few essentials, then he was out the door. He started the bike and backed it out of the crowded apartment garage, gunned the motor, and sped off with nothing but a cheap helmet and his wallet.

For miles there were no obstacles, and Aidriel began to think that maybe he'd slipped past them, and was home free. It was such a surprise to see the little girl Passer crouching in the middle of the open country road outside Clinton that he had no time to react. The spirit materialized out of thin air only moments before he drove by, holding some kind of long metal spike. He swerved around it, and the Passer turned. As if in slow motion, Aidriel watched the small hand rise and swing down, colliding with the blur of his front tire with inhuman strength. There was a sound like a small explosion, and he was suddenly thrown forward. As if incapable of detangling himself, Aidriel's hands and legs clung to the motorcycle in a death grip. He

123

rolled across the road, the bike spinning with him, and every inch of his body collided with something.

Somehow, he landed on his side in the ditch, the bike lying on top of one of his legs and his torso. He tried to stir or turn his head, but couldn't seem to break through the curtain of pain shrouding his being. His other leg was bent back, probably broken, and neither arm was responding to his conscious efforts to move them.

Aidriel could hear cars passing on the road, though none of them slowed. The ditch was not that deep; could no one see him? He wanted to yell out, but all that he could manage was a cross between a bitter laugh and sob of pain. The bike was hot against his side, and was searing through his clothing. He could feel the terrible scorching pain and smelled burning, but was entirely helpless.

He had no idea how long he had laid there before Rubin walked down and stood beside him, pulling the lifesaving helmet off his head and staring in disgust.

"I've found you," the Passer said.

"How do you do that?" Aidriel did not recognize his own shell-shocked voice.

"'Do'?"

"Send messages to the other Passers to stop me?"

"They know you're coming."

Aidriel gasped and repeated his earlier cry of dismay. He was in so much pain, it was unreal. His nerves were on fire; he knew there would be burns on his side.

"You bring this on yourself," Rubin snarled, bending over to talk in Aidriel's face as it did when he was a kid. "You're *selfish*! You think of only yourself and how things affect *you*!"

"What choice do you give me?" Aidriel groaned, trying with little success to shift out from under the scorching surface of the motorcycle. "I have to spend all my time trying to survive and stay one step ah…"

Aidriel was beginning to lose consciousness, but was terrified that if he did, Rubin would finish him off.

He saw his Passer straighten, toss aside the helmet and calmly climb the side of the ditch to the street, motioning at an approaching car to stop. As the vehicle slowed, a woman in the passenger seat stuck her head out of the window and craned her neck, spotting the crashed sportbike and its rider. Darting back inside the car, she spoke hurriedly and with concern to the driver about calling for help.

Aidriel realized as he began to gain minimal control of his movements, that when he turned his head slightly, he could see the little girl Passer standing on the far side of the ditch, just out of his range of view when he was limp. He wondered why the spirit had remained still and quiet while he lay at its mercy.

Seeing that he was aware of it, the Passer spoke, but its small voice was drowned out by Aidriel's involuntary moans of pain. Too weary to pay any attention to his surroundings, Aidriel laid his head down in the damp grass and tried to find some semblance of relief. The child Passer walked down and around him slowly, stopping right in front of his head. He could see the detail of its ghostly lace-trimmed socks and Mary-Jane shoes.

"I'm sorry," the little girl whispered, and kicked him in the face.

The second time Aidriel awoke in the rental car, he was sore from sitting in the same position for an extended period of time, and wondered how long he had been asleep. He shifted and blinked, feeling more awake and aware from the rest and the wearing-off medication. The clock must be wrong; it said it was four hours since they left. The GPS was turned off.

Dreamer was more relaxed and was bobbing her head in time to an upbeat Katy Perry song on the radio, which she'd turned up again. She was smiling and tapping her fingers against the wheel, observing their surroundings.

Sitting up straighter, Aidriel looked out the windows and saw that they were driving on a long, straight stretch of suburban highway with no car in sight in either direction. They slowed down through a little town with a firehouse and a cemetery, then only houses and country roads passed on either side.

With a sinking feeling, Aidriel tried to make sense of the scene. Perhaps the clock wasn't incorrect after all. He had no idea where they were, but it was most definitely not the airport or expressway. And Williams's car was no longer following them.

"Where are we?" he asked gruffly.

Dreamer turned and smiled, her eyes remarkably lucid and her movements relaxed.

"Just west of Toledo," she said.

Toledo was not supposed to be one of the stops on the ride. In fact, Toledo was beyond the airport—way beyond.

"Why are…?" Aidriel was too bewildered to form an articulate question.

Dreamer smiled mischievously.

"I lost them," she said with a shrug. "I got far enough ahead and took the wrong exit. I've been weaving around since then to make sure they won't find us."

Aidriel stared at her, even more confused. Lost them? Lost who? Williams and deTarlo? Why in the world would Dreamer intentionally get them lost in an unfamiliar state in an unfamiliar vehicle? What if the Passers caused them to crash? The whole reasoning behind Aidriel riding separately and ahead of Williams and deTarlo was so that if something happened to him, they would know and could handle it.

"*Why* did you lose them intentionally?" he demanded, punching the button on the stereo to turn it off. His immediate impression was of how incredibly stupid Dreamer was. This was not at all how he had imagined she would help him. He was angry he had trusted her to drive, and disappointed because he liked her and kind of trusted her. Now she'd gone and made such a thoughtless decision without asking him, and they might both be in danger because of it.

Dreamer became very nervous and kept her lips sealed, her eyes on the road. Her knuckles began to whiten as she gripped the wheel.

"Because I thought *you* wanted to lose them," she mumbled finally. "You were upset with how blasé they were being about your safety, but you'd

127

signed deTarlo's papers, so I figured this was your only way out."

"Why would you make a decision like this without asking me first?" Aidriel demanded angrily.

The strain between them was intensifying, and Dreamer refused to look at him, keeping her gaze fixed on the open road. Another car flew past from the opposite direction, and she tilted her head down, her eyes following it as it passed. She was taking on the appearance of a frightened child being reprimanded, and were she not driving the car, she probably would be considering giving in to her flight reflex.

"I'm sorry," Dreamer whispered.

"What good does that do us?" snapped Aidriel. "We're lost and hours away from the airport. Either they've left without us or are lost somewhere looking for us and you've cost us hours."

Dreamer was leaning away from Aidriel, gripping the wheel as if for dear life. She was pushing her foot down on the accelerator without realizing it and they were increasing in speed, flying past the crops in the fields on either side of the road in a blur.

Arriving at a stop sign, she stomped on the brake a little too late and they jerked to a halt. Looking left and right only once, Dreamer clicked on her blinker and whirled left, once more gunning the engine to get up to speed. She still wouldn't look at Aidriel.

"Pull over," he ordered, sitting up straighter in his seat and itching to grab the wheel out of her hands. Dreamer said nothing, but showed no signs of doing as he wished.

128

"Pull over," he repeated harshly. "I'm driving."

"No," she answered, her voice low and uncertain. "You don't know where we are."

"Well, I'll use the GPS and actually do what it says," he shot back, his voice rising in irritation.

Dreamer didn't flinch and continued driving at her own speed. Aidriel was becoming increasingly aggravated that she refused to listen to him. The thought that he could not control her made him wish he could get rid of her, his mind filling in the word *divorce* for some reason.

"Pull over," he ordered again, his temper and volume rising.

Dreamer took in a deep breath, flying through an intersection at the fastest speed she dared.

"No, I'm driving," she answered. "If I get out, you'll leave without me."

Aidriel flinched at the painful memories stirred by her words.

"Why would I leave without you?"

"Because you're mad, I don't know. But if I get out, you might drive away without me and leave me here on my own."

Abandonment was not something to cite so thoughtlessly. In his anger, Aidriel assumed Dreamer had no experience with such a thing; she should never have mentioned it.

"That's so stupid!" he exclaimed. She was accusing him of being more selfish and inconsiderate than *she* seemed to be, and his pride was hurt. If she believed her claim so strongly that she refused to stop, there was no way for him to prove her wrong.

"I'm not stupid," Dreamer answered defensively.

"I didn't say *you* were stupid."

"Not in those words, you didn't."

"Well, stop making stupid decisions if you want me to think you're not! Why'd you go and get us lost?"

"Why not?" Dreamer shot back, finally looking at him. "Where were we even going? To another Bird Cage? Back to Fort Wayne? Does it matter where they were taking you? Nothing good was going to happen, if anything changed at all!"

"You consider this a good change?"

"None of the Passers have attacked us yet. Keeping ahead of them isn't a bad thing."

Aidriel thought that he'd rather be somewhere familiar when the Passers did find him, but held his tongue. What *was* the difference where he was? The attacks were no less brutal based on where he was, so why *not* drive down some random road in the middle of nowhere?

Perhaps it was a sense of obligation to make good on his agreement and the helplessness of decisions being made without his input. Dreamer's choice to take him away from Williams and deTarlo was no different than deTarlo's choice to send him to Kelly Road. He didn't have a say in either resolution, and it felt worse now that someone he considered a peer and not an authority was choosing for him.

"You are not making any more decisions," he said finally in a steely tone. "You're just the phlebotomist."

"And you're just the patient," she answered, upset at being slighted like that again. "Besides, you were asleep. You could have driven *yourself*."

Aidriel didn't care to answer and looked out the window as they rolled up to another light, waiting for it to become green before Dreamer turned right. They passed a giant steel plant on the left with a billowing cloud of steam and followed closely behind a slow semitruck for several minutes before a town came into sight.

It suddenly passed from Aidriel's mind how upset he was to realize he liked traveling. He had not been able to afford much sojourning in his youth, and after the attacks from the Passers began, he had stopped entirely. Frustration had long since changed to despair when even the thought of leaving Fort Wayne entered his mind. But once he had been taken to Kelly Road and had long hours alone, he'd realized how little that trip had mattered. Yes, he was out of state, finally. But he was inside a featureless dome; he might as well have never left home.

This, however, was different. The landscape was not remarkably unlike what he was used to, but the particulars of this town were foreign. He saw shops he had not seen in Indiana. And he was not the one driving. Aidriel could not remember the last time he was a passenger and was not being attacked by the spirits he saw all around. But now they didn't even glance his way.

Dreamer brought up the GPS and had it search for a hotel, following the directions through a light, past a Walmart and Mexican restaurant, then turning right again on State Route 108. Still the awkward silence ensued until Dreamer switched the radio back on. After half a song, they arrived at a several-story hotel on the left, and Dreamer parked a bit faster than required.

Once the car was off, the two sat in silence, staring out the windows. Dreamer shifted and looked at Aidriel, swallowing, and softly offered an apology.

"I'm not mad at you," he replied.

"You were a bit ago."

Aidriel just shrugged and focused his attention on her. There were circles under her eyes. He hadn't once thought of how tired she must be, or that she was probably just as sore from the ambulance crash as he was. It had been on his mind how lost and disconnected he was, but she was in exactly the same boat. She was a girl in a strange town with a strange man. It hadn't quite dawned on him before now how they were actually one another's responsibility, however they each interpreted it. To the best of his ability, he should protect her.

"I'm not mad at you," he repeated.

Dreamer just nodded and became uncomfortable, pinching the soft surface of the wheel with her nails.

Aidriel held out his hand.

"Give me the card," he said. "I'll get us a room."

Without a word, Dreamer leaned toward the door to reach into the side pocket of her scrub top. Her fingers brushed the palm of Aidriel's hand when she put the credit card in it. He got out and walked away from her toward the building.

Dreamer rested her elbow against the door, supporting her head on her hand. She closed her eyes to rest and wait, and felt the sudden drop in temperature. An adolescent girl Passer with pale hair was sitting patiently in the seat beside her, watching. Dreamer started in surprise.

"Dreamer?" said the ghost in a strange, monotone voice. "My name is Maralyn."

"You don't know me; I've never seen you before."

"You never will again. I follow another. We speak to each other; every one."

"Who does?"

"The Passersby."

Dreamer looked toward the hotel, hoping Aidriel wouldn't come out.

"What do you want?" she asked.

Maralyn began to sob, and cradled its face in its hands.

"It's going to be worse for him," it mumbled. "I'm warning you to be ready. If my words could help you, would you listen to them? You mustn't let him go."

"Stay away from this hotel," Dreamer said in a threatening tone. Maralyn looked up sadly and nodded.

"Answer it," it blubbered. Dreamer promptly opened the door, taking the keys from the ignition and getting out of the car. As she was walking toward the building, the phone in her pocket began to ring. She took it out with a wary glance over her shoulder, but she couldn't tell if Maralyn was still in the car. Dreamer looked at the display; she didn't want to talk to him right now. Besides, she was disinclined to do as the Passer told her. She put the phone back into her pocket and pushed through the hotel door.

****

It is not often that someone with a gift is the only one of their kind in the world, which was true of Chester Williams. He had a gift to see the invisible Passers, but he knew of two others like him, and none of them assumed they were the only three.

In Moscow, there was a college student in his mid-twenties named Tosya, who could also always see Passers, though he was not affiliated with the official Russian Sentience organization.

Tosya had Williams's personal cell number, and spoke English well enough to carry on conversations in it; Chester knew very little Russian. It was no surprise to Williams to receive a call from Tosya out of the blue. Telling deTarlo and his assistant to cease their semi-panicked conversation about losing Dreamer and Aidriel, Chester turned his complete attention to his phone.

"Do you know what is happening?" asked the Russian.

"What do you mean?"

"Why do the Passers move? In crowds?"

Chester hesitated as he tried to translate the meaning of the questions.

"Many Passers are moving," Tosya clarified. "Crowds of them, walking without words across the lands and into the sea."

"They're migrating?"

Now Tosya was lost and paused to think.

"Are *all* Passers going?" asked Chester. "Flocking like birds? Following a silent signal, like compass needles turning toward a magnetic pole?"

134

"Yes," Tosya agreed. "Not just here, but in all of Asia and Europe, I have heard."

"I've been isolated," Chester started to make excuses.

"I called Dorotéia," Tosya continued. "It is the same in South America. Longer than it has been here."

The third of those gifted with special sight, Dorotéia was a Brazilian woman in her forties. Like Tosya, she was not officially associated with any organization, but she stayed very current on Passer events. Chester wondered why she had not called him, if she knew about this migration before either he or Tosya did.

"Why didn't she get in touch with me?" Williams asked. "It's been going on in Brazil longer than there?"

Tosya answered with an affirmative.

"Seas of Passers go through the cities," he said. "Have you not seen this?"

Chester looked out the window of the car, and though he could see Passers, none of them were "migrating."

"No, I'll look into it."

"Okay," Tosya agreed. "*Do svidaniya.*"

Chester laid his phone on his lap and continued to stare out the window, bewildered.

Dreamer was relieved to see that Maralyn had left when she and Aidriel went back out to the car to get the two tubs of supplies from the trunk. The phlebotomist found it bizarre that Aidriel was suddenly as chivalrous as possible, ensuring that he carried the heavier carton. Their room was in the back corner of the top floor, as far from other guests—and their Passers—as possible. It was the middle of the week, fortunately, so the hotel was mostly empty.

It made Dreamer nervous that they were sharing a single room, but she thought it was probably safer that way. Aidriel unlocked the door with the keycard and held it open for her. She shyly thanked him and set down her tub, taking in the room.

"Which bed do you want?" she asked.

Aidriel set his container on top of hers and looked at the beds thoughtfully for a moment, then studied her face before he answered.

"Why don't we push the beds together?" he suggested.

Dreamer wasn't sure how to answer and stared back at him, watching for a hint of sarcasm or teasing. He appeared to be serious.

"Uh, why?" she mumbled.

"They're…small," he said.

"They're doubles. That's not too small."

"I think we should push them together."

Dreamer was becoming uncomfortable with where the discussion was going, especially since she couldn't detect any hint of jest in his face or voice.

"You want the beds to be right next to each other…," she clarified.

"Yep."

"So it's one big bed?"

"Right."

"So you want to…share…a bed." It made Dreamer blush to say it. The corners of Aidriel's mouth turned up so slightly it was barely perceptible, but he nodded.

"Yes."

"I don't think that's a good idea," stammered Dreamer.

She saw the flash of disappointment in his eyes as he turned away, shrugging as if he didn't care. The phleb was astounded and confused. A short time ago, Aidriel was yelling at her and insinuating that she was stupid, and now he was suggesting they become cozy. She just couldn't understand him.

"I'll take that one," Aidriel said, pointing toward the further bed. "I don't want to be between you and the door, in case you need to get out."

His wording made Dreamer shudder, but she didn't argue. Nothing else was said while they set out the supplies to their liking, Aidriel looking carefully around the room while Dreamer went through the tubs to see what clothing had been sent along with them. None of their personal belongings had been packed, but a set of scrubs and plain clothes for each of them had been. Her set of jeans and a long-sleeved shirt matched the one he was currently wearing. Dreamer smiled slightly; that was most likely not intentional.

In the bottom of one of the containers was a grouping of uninteresting essentials, including soaps, toothbrushes, tissues, and the like. As Dreamer began to take out and arrange the items in a tidy cluster on the sink beneath the large mirror, Aidriel plopped onto his back on his bed, clasping his hands behind his head.

"You tired?" asked Dreamer from the bathroom alcove.

"No. We should have food delivered."

"Alright. You need any pills?"

"No. What should we eat?"

"Whatever you would like, as long as it's not seafood."

CHAPTER 9

Dr. Ana deTarlo ignored the stares of Williams's staff and flight crew as she paced up and down the asphalt of the tarmac next to the car. Her cell phone was glued to her ear and her heels clicked severely. She'd called everyone she could think to, and was getting nowhere.

"Why don't you just ask the Passers where they are?" she had demanded of Chester earlier when they realized they had lost Dreamer and Aidriel. Williams was sitting in the front passenger seat of the car, tapping furiously on his tablet device.

"I'll ask Rod when it finds us, and Kara," he answered without looking back. "But they might not know where they went either. Even if the Passers did know, they wouldn't tell us. I don't think the spirits want us anywhere near the guy."

Williams had been receiving important phone calls himself, and had boarded the plane to use a more comfortable environment while he worked. He would get off the line with one of his employees just to have another call and tell him the same news. They'd been trying to get a hold of him since the story broke.

"Tell deTarlo to get on board right now," he told his assistant, his phone lowered against his neck as he was still on the line. He hadn't taken the time to locate his Bluetooth earpiece.

It had required one of the security guards to get involved before Ana reluctantly obeyed and clambered precariously up the steps to the plane.

"We can't just leave without them," she argued immediately. "What if they just got lost?"

"Shut up," Chester hushed her, focusing his attention back on his call. With an icy glare, deTarlo stood over him and waited impatiently for an explanation. When he finally hung up with a troubled sigh, she demanded, "Well?"

"Within the last twenty-four hours," Williams explained sullenly, "a strange migration of Passers has begun in Asia, Europe and South America, possibly the other continents as well. Seems that *all* the spirits are inexplicably disappearing entirely or abandoning their charges and heading for the U.S."

It didn't appear to sink in for deTarlo at first, and she just stared at him without speaking.

"What does this sound like to you?" he asked. "Things turn intense for our guy after the sentinel event, and all of a sudden, Passers are becoming violently bipolar and are now traveling great distances to get here."

"Are you telling me that every single ghost on the planet is coming here after Aidriel Akimos?"

Chester looked grim, a flash of panic setting his eyes aflame.

"If they do," he said, "that will be over a billion Passers converging on a single person. He'll be like a piece of tissue paper in a hurricane."

Stunned, deTarlo sank into a chair and let the hand gripping her cell phone flop into her lap. What could be done? She desperately wished Dreamer would answer her cell phone, or that they could somehow warn Aidriel about what was coming. It was truly meltdown worthy, but the shrink calmly took her clipboard out of her shoulder bag and began writing feverishly. Her report had to hit the press before this happened. Soon, the entire world would hang on her every word.

Dr. St. Cross leaned his elbow on the arm of his wheelchair with his head in his hand, his green eyes tensely following the movements of Todd, a thirty-something male nurse barely out of school. Andrei looked on from nearby, harboring a similar annoyance toward Todd, but for a different reason. The nurse was not a believer in taking Passers' word as gospel.

St. Cross had known Todd's parents for years; they used to be neighbors. Todd was a nice enough guy, and was eager to accept the psychiatrist's request for private employment for the duration of the planned trip while the nurse was looking for a permanent job. But Todd could be pushy and overbearing, in an endearing way, and had no problem with telling the wheelchair-bound older man how things were.

"You don't need so many books," Todd had insisted, scooping an armload of them out of St. Cross's suitcase and dumping them on the bed. The shrink had winced at the harsh treatment, but uncomplainingly bit his tongue. It was driving him crazy how untidy Todd's packing of his clothing was; everything would be wrinkled.

Todd paused importantly after stacking the suitcase and medical case by the door. He crossed his arms and looked around the kitchen of the house, stroking his goatee and pretending St. Cross and Andrei weren't there.

"Okay, we're ready," he finally said without bothering to consult the shrink. He glanced at his watch, muttering something about having plenty of time to catch the plane. St. Cross still did not complain and began to wheel his chair toward the door.

"Just wait here," Todd said, holding out his hand in a stop motion. "I'll take the stuff out to the car and come back."

St. Cross stopped and waited. He had to implement some of his calming techniques to tolerate the younger man. Taking out his mobile, he checked for messages and was disappointed not to find any.

"My friend," Andrei said suddenly, "perhaps you should take with you your case, the one in the bedside table."

St. Cross looked to his Passer's face, wondering why the ghost would tell him to bring that. Was it possible Aidriel would need it? The shrink was doubtful. But there was no denying Andrei's ability to glimpse into the future. There was a reason behind its suggestion.

The psychiatrist wheeled down the corridor and into his bedroom, taking a magazine organizer–size plastic case out of his nightstand drawer and bringing it back into the kitchen on his lap.

Todd returned, and seeing the case, asked, "What's that?"

"Absolutely essential," answered St. Cross.

With a charitable shrug, Todd took the handles of the wheelchair and pushed it out the door, closing it on Andrei. The Passer stopped angrily for a moment before stepping through the wood panel and following them across the porch and down the ramp.

"I saw some of my medical record on deTarlo's clipboard," Aidriel said, poking holes in his foam food tray with his fork. "I noticed something about a 'sentinel event.' What is that?"

Dreamer dabbed at her lips with a paper napkin before she answered.

"Usually it means some unexpected injury, illness or death of a patient while in a hospital's care, like surgery on a wrong part of the body or a baby that dies for no apparent reason. I think in your case, it refers to your suicide attempt, since it was less than seventy-two hours after you left the hospital last time."

"Oh." Aidriel thought for a moment and stabbed at his ravioli.

"I heard Mr. Williams talking about it with a doctor," Dreamer continued. "They consider the increase of hostility toward you after Mr. Watts's death a sentinel event also. It's kind of like an illness spread to you while you were under their care, only it was, I don't know, a mental illness."

Aidriel made a face of disagreement but didn't answer. He and Dreamer were sitting across from each other at the little table in their room, the Italian food they'd ordered from a pizza place between them. The sun was nearly set outside and they'd kept the curtains closed and turned on the lights. The remote for the television was lying at the foot of Aidriel's bed where he'd left it after

143

handling it earlier while debating whether to turn the TV on; he'd elected not to.

"How much does Dr. deTarlo discuss with you about your records?" Dreamer asked with a casual flick of her gaze at him.

"No one discusses anything with me," Aidriel answered, eating a raviolo. Dreamer just nodded and waited.

"So how long have you been working at the hospital?" he asked her. "I don't think I've ever seen you before."

"Only a couple of weeks," she answered. "I was a contingent, but one of the other girls is on maternity leave so I was working in her place. I also worked at a Coma Center."

"That's one of those hospitals for brain-dead people, right?"

"Sort of. Most of the patients are actually still alive in the brain, just indefinitely unconscious. Like from car accidents and stuff. I liked it; it was nice and quiet. They'd play classical or mood music, and kept the lights pretty low. I worked third shift, so I was never there when the families visited. I didn't have to draw much blood, either, so I spent a lot of time reading. They just had a staff of medical workers for any possible scenario."

Aidriel listened and simply nodded. He liked the way she carefully cut her Alfredo noodles into small, manageable bites with her plastic fork and knife and made him wait for her answers so she wouldn't talk with her mouth full. It somehow made the disposable dishes from which they ate seem ridiculously cheap.

"You don't work there anymore?" Aidriel asked about the Coma Center. Chewing, Dreamer shook her head.

"I was technically still an employee when I switched to the hospital. Since it was third shift, and the hospital was first, I went straight from one to the other, and pretty much spent any time off work sleeping. I had weekends off, though, and it was only going to be until the other girl got back from leave, so it wasn't too big of a deal. And the Coma Center wasn't a demanding job. I quit them both to work for Williams."

"Why'd you do that?" There was a hint of guilt in Aidriel's voice.

Dreamer watched him for hidden signals for a moment, waiting because they both knew at least part of the answer. Finally she shrugged and went back to eating.

"Better money," she said simply.

Aidriel wondered if she was lying just so he wouldn't feel like a total jerk.

"What about you?" Dreamer asked. "Where do you work?"

He had to think briefly before answering.

"My last job was at a gift store. You'd think it'd be a pretty safe place to work, but I had two heavy framed pictures and a glass statuette fall off the shelves on me. The last one cracked me open, and they thought I was just a klutz and fired me."

He tilted his head forward and pointed to a recent scar on the top of his skull, barely visible under his hair. Dreamer swallowed hard and appeared troubled.

"How many times have you been to the hospital?" she asked.

"Too many times to remember. I don't really want to dredge anything up."

The phlebotomist looked uncomfortable for asking and quickly nodded, remembering patient privacy. Neither spoke and finished their food awkwardly. Aidriel pushed his foam dish aside and stuffed a stick of gum into his mouth. Leaning his elbow on the table, he rested his head against the knuckles of his fist, watching Dreamer. She quickly stood, collecting everything from the table and carrying it to the garbage can under the sink. Shyly refusing to look at him, she gathered clean clothes from the plastic storage tub and asked, "You mind if I shower?"

Without lifting his head from his hand, Aidriel shook it no, and Dreamer retreated into the bathroom. He sat still and listened to the water turn on, then indifferently got to his feet and paced the room. Three times he wandered from one end to the other, picking up the remote, pausing in thought, and putting it down again, finally finding himself at the window. Pulling aside the curtain, Aidriel looked out into the twilight, at the line of houses directly behind the hotel. There was no activity that he could make out, though several of the windows were illuminated in light. He didn't see any Passers, and was relieved, at least for the moment.

The familiar thought came to Aidriel: when he lay down tonight to sleep, he might be awakened by an attack. Just the possibility made his nerves tingle with dread, and he asked himself if he were to die, would he be ready? He had thought he was ready weeks ago when he tossed the rope over the ceiling hook in the living room in his apartment. The former owners had a hammock chair hanging from

146

the hook, so he had known it would support his weight. It was strange how fondly he recalled that rope. Did he wish for it again? Would he like to die tonight?

The lights in one of the houses below went out one room at a time as the occupants retired to sleep. Aidriel tried to think of what he still wanted to see or do before he died, in case the Passers would kill him soon. Every night could be his last night. The only good thing that had happened to him since his attempted hanging was that a girl had come into his life. A girl that he felt a connection to, however slight, and was beginning to feel affection for. He wouldn't want her to be the one to find him if he were to die, and wondered if that meant that he really liked her.

Having come to the conclusion that Dreamer needed him and relied on him made Aidriel experience a sense as familiar as a memory, but entirely new to him. In his youth he'd gone through the usual teen stage of feeling he could take on the world and was impervious to anything as long as he wished to be. But all his dreams of grandeur had vanished when the attacks began and he'd been broken ever since. Having Dreamer with him, shielding him in the small way she could and relying on him for protection in return, he felt like he had reached the stage of maturity he had been cheated out of. She was strong, he suspected, but she was still a woman, and being with her made him a man. He was a target and a patient, but above all—most importantly, he reminded himself—he was a man and should act like one. The most basic aspect of fulfillment was accepting the weight of manly responsibility; a whole world might open before him if he would step up to face it, as Dreamer's very presence was inspiring him to do.

For some reason, he imagined he was standing close to Dreamer, their fingers interlaced, her head resting against his collarbone, and his pulse began to pound like it did when he was afraid. There was no accompanying pain or fear; he must really like her.

Aidriel was letting his mind wander to what he'd like to do with her and was startled back to the present when Dreamer shut off the water in the bathroom. He continued to wait, his ears attuned to the slightest sounds she made. Presently, she opened the bathroom door and came out, her wet hair a tousled mess. She stood before the mirror over the sink and pulled a brush through the tangles, after carefully folding and stowing her clothes from the day.

Aidriel watched her reflection in the mirror but pretended he wasn't whenever she turned from it. She was round-faced, and her most attractive feature was her feminine lips, though there were varying shades of color in her glaucous irises. Aidriel hoped she was a little older than she looked.

He continued to follow her movements with his eyes until she stopped and began to rearrange the bottles on the sink, smoothing down the hand towel. Picking up his discarded gum wrapper from the table, he took it over to the garbage, leaning over beside Dreamer to put it and the gum in the trash. As he straightened, he leaned in toward her, his hand resting on the small of her back and his face nearly touching her head as he breathed in the sweet scent of the shampoo in her hair.

Dreamer instantly shrunk away from him, slipping sideways to take several defensive steps into the room.

"What're you doing?" she asked, embarrassed. Aidriel took a step toward her and she drew back.

"Your hair smells good," he said. Dreamer nervously tucked it behind her ears and looked away.

"Well, thanks...," she mumbled, unsure how to respond. Aidriel took another step toward her.

"*You* smell good," he said, his gray eyes fixed keenly on her face. She was becoming very anxious and he wanted to reassure her, but it didn't feel to him like the right time to back down. She blushed, which struck him as wholly appealing; he was immensely magnetized and advanced further.

Dreamer's hand shot out defensively as if to block him and she said, "No, I don't think..." Her voice trailed off and she once again widened the gap between them. "I don't know you very well."

Aidriel smiled and put his hands in his pockets. "Does that matter?"

"Yes, it does."

They were watching each other very closely for the slightest of cues, but neither moved. Aidriel beckoned with his eyes, and the teetering Dreamer felt between surrender and resistance played out on her face. Her gaze gave way beneath his and focused on his arm at his side, squinting in close scrutiny before slowly blinking. She shook her head and pressed her fingertips against her forehead as if in pain.

"There're no Passers around," Aidriel said. "No one to get between us."

"There'll be...nothing to get between."

"Why not?" Aidriel flashed his most winning smile, and saw her lips instinctively curve in response. It looked hard for her to speak.

"I don't think it's a good idea," she managed. "It wouldn't be smart for us to act on something that could be so heartbreaking. We've only known each other for a few days."

"Well I *want* to know you." Aidriel advanced again, but she remained where she was. Her hands began wringing nervously, and he wanted to take them in his and make them stop. He wanted to seize her before she could get away again and pull her toward him, but he restrained himself.

"No…," she started to insist when he whispered her name.

"I could die tonight." Aidriel's answer was both a plea and an excuse. "It's tough to go with your instincts. You learn to live every day like it's your last."

"That could make you really selfish, though."

"It makes you prioritize," he answered.

Dreamer had stopped fidgeting and was once again holding eye contact with him. He got the feeling she was trying to communicate that there was something she had realized about him that was making her oppose his advances, but he didn't care to let her solve the puzzle of conveying it. Women always wanted to make things about emotions and connections and protecting hearts, but he wasn't interested. There was no point in thinking about or rationalizing something so simple; he wanted to act on how she made him feel.

She melted when he whispered her name again, stepping closer to her. Still she didn't move, and when he came within touching distance, she lowered her head a little and closed her eyes, waiting. Aidriel gently closed his fingers around her wrists and touched her shoulder with his, leaning in so his nose brushed her cheek. Dreamer shook her head faintly.

It drove Aidriel crazy that she was resisting in action. He could have sworn she drew slightly nearer to him. His heart was thumping again, and almost felt as if hers was beating in unison. It took all of his self-control to not kiss her, and resisting made his desire to do so intensely stronger. He closed his eyes and savored an emotion beside fear, a pleasant buzzing in his senses much stronger than dread. He didn't want to die tonight, so long as the feeling lasted.

But a sense of the pain that would result if he continued prevailed upon him for the briefest of moments; some notion that the ultimate cost to them would be too high. Aidriel's lips brushed Dreamer's cheek, but he let go of her and stepped back, taking a deep breath. Their eyes opened and looked to each other, and she smiled. He instantly hated himself for withdrawing, but it was too late to kiss her now. Stopping himself was an instinctual reaction to impending trouble, but moreover a subconscious choice to alter the course of his near future, simply because he could. It was empowering for something to be at his command.

"There're scrubs for you in the tote," she said.

His nerves still buzzing, Aidriel grabbed the clothes from the storage tub and locked himself into the bathroom, gradually recognizing what he had cheated himself out of. He threw the black apparel onto the floor in disappointment, yanking the faucet on. Switching it to shower, he held his head under the cold water, ignoring how it drenched the collar of his shirt.

Dreamer got into bed and laid on her side, listening to the water running and trying to relax enough to fall asleep. She was a bit shaken but was smiling. She had indeed been conflicted when he was holding her wrists, hoping he'd kiss her but praying he wouldn't. To her it seemed his sudden desire for intimacy would prove harmful; perhaps a whiplash reaction to the scene they had set for themselves, and a playing-out of some unseen script written for them by the actions of others. There was no reason anything should happen.

Dreamer had no psychological training, but she thought Aidriel was too cynical and unhappy to be attracted to her. Giving in to his advances might have afforded him a temporary thrill, but would only compound his emotional damage when it was over and they realized that they were nobody to each other. Yes, Dreamer was increasingly drawn to him, but she had no idea if he was genuinely reciprocating. While he was pushing the boundaries of his safety where the Passers were concerned, she was balanced on her own edge of allowed actions, riskily close to crossing a line she knew she shouldn't. If she were acting on a plan of any sort regarding him, which she wasn't, he'd probably be exactly where she wanted him. She'd had her share of relationships; nothing serious, but she had learned that small things could make an impact. A few sly smiles, a coy invitation in the eyes, a slow wetting of her lips, and he might go crazy. He was damaged; it was unfair to play games with him, even if he started them.

When Aidriel got out of the shower, Dreamer was propped up on her pillows, reading a paperback. He turned off all the lights but the one above her, tossing his clothes thoughtlessly into the bin. Plopping backward on his bed as he had done earlier, he locked his fingers behind his damp head. She read on in silence, distracted by him; he stared at the ceiling.

Aidriel began to earnestly sing Sting's *Be Still My Beating Heart* as if he were alone. Dreamer smiled and laid down her book, rolling to her side to prop her head up on her hand, listening to him sing the chorus, second verse and bridge. As he repeated the chorus and let his voice fade away, Dreamer reached up and turned off the light.

Dr. St. Cross was not partial to snakes himself, though he found it fascinating and soothing to watch them gliding over the network of branches he had placed in his aquarium at home. It was because of Andrei that he kept the reptiles at all. His Passer had come to him at the beginning of the Sentience, and had proved to be an intelligent, gentle companion, most of the time. Andrei died overseas, but it was not bizarre that it had found its way back to the States to keep company with St. Cross; Passers were often found great distances from where they had died, just as many were bound to a location by an invisible chain.

Andrei had been bitten by a snake, and had succumbed to the venom. This was not long before the Passersby stepped into everyday life. Andrei was a lover of adventure when he was still alive, and had traveled far and wide. While exploring the jungles of India, foolishly without a guide, he had come upon the snake without seeing it. He stepped too close, and the strike was delivered to his thigh. Unwisely electing to attempt to run to civilization for help, Andrei had only quickened the spread of the poison in his blood. He had died alone and in agony, lying in the undergrowth; his body was never discovered by humans.

But somehow, it comforted the Passer to wander a house in which the cause of its death was a harmless display to entertain the eye. None of St. Cross's snakes were poisonous, but as a psychiatrist, he understood Andrei's need to have the creatures near.

"Does it give you a sense of security to see them caged?" he asked the Passer once.

"No, I need to make peace with them," was the response. "To make peace with my death, as it were."

Passers only remained among the living while their souls were unfulfilled. St. Cross assumed, then, that because Andrei was still present, the peace had not yet been made.

CHAPTER 10

In the darkest, quietest hour of the night, Dreamer was awakened to her bed shaking. Her first thought was of Aidriel, and she was seriously preparing to deck him in the face if he tried anything. But before she was fully awake, the rough feeling of a body climbing over her filled her with terror. The next one that climbed over was in such a hurry she was thrown right off the bed and onto the floor between it and the wall. She cried out.

It was pitch-black in the room, but lying facedown on the carpet, Dreamer could see gray and white movement out of the corner of her eye. If Aidriel was already awake, he made no sound, and she couldn't hear anything until he slammed suddenly into the wall on the other side of the room. There were repeated thuds of something, possibly his head, striking the wall, and the shuffling of the sheets of his bed. He suddenly took a short, deep breath, as if he had been under water.

The strong smell of electrical burning hung in the air and something was hissing and sputtering. Dreamer turned her head as far as she could toward the wall and saw the feet of a Passer mere inches away. As if it could sense her notice, it paused in its movement to lean over, its face sweeping down close to hers. The wide empty eyes stared through her, the lips arching in a snarl. The ghost almost seemed to be taking deliberate, angry inhales. Closing her eyes, the phlebotomist got swiftly up, untangling herself from the blankets.

The Passers coming through the front wall and converging on the small area between Aidriel's bed and the far end of the room were so numerous, Dreamer couldn't see through their ghostly forms. The television and temperature unit under the window were sparking and smoking. The room was bitterly cold and she shivered, scrambling up onto the bed. The Passers shoved her forward, tumbling her to the floor again on the other side, by the nightstand and between the beds.

Dreamer was stunned and at first lay still, covering her face with her hands. She had never seen so many Passers before, neither had she been so harshly dealt with, besides when they scratched her at the hospital. She could hear Aidriel manage another gasp for breath, and realized he was probably being choked or smothered. It was frightening how deliberate and silent the ghosts were.

There were two more thumps against the far wall, and Aidriel managed to shout for her to run. But she had to help him; the Passers were out for blood.

Dreamer reached under the skirt of his bed, and her hand collided with a board of wood. She couldn't get to him under it; she'd have to climb over. Without allowing herself to even think, she got up and let the Passers shove her onto the bed as they flowed forward. Clinging to the bedding, she

156

reached over the side into the ghostly blur. Her hand groped and she held her breath, but she found fabric, clutched it, and pulled.

Aidriel rolled to the side, possible against his will, and Dreamer's fingers lost their grasp. The angry spirits flung her back off the bed to the floor. In a fright, she got up and ran to the door, slamming into the wall and flicking on the light switch. Some of the Passers seemed startled by the sudden flood of light and withdrew, but the majority continued their attack, unbothered.

Looking across the foggy room, Dreamer was surprised to see the scrubs Aidriel had been wearing as pajamas lying in a heap on the carpet. She was afraid to draw close to help, but remembered she'd felt fabric when she grabbed onto him. The top supplies tub had been overturned on the floor, and his clothing was no longer inside it; even his shoes were missing. He must have sensed the attack coming and had gotten dressed in hopes of escaping.

Without another thought, Dreamer threw herself forward into the fray, yelling for the Passers to let go of Aidriel and let him breathe. To her surprise, the ghosts appeared startled by her. They rose to turn and stare, temporarily ceasing the assault. Had they never been directly addressed during previous attacks?

Gasping for air, Aidriel used the bed for support as he dragged himself to his feet. He fell back against the wall, bruised and scratched, holding his throat in pain. Dreamer found herself standing dumbly at the foot of his bed, watching all the angry ghosts that stared back, many of them finally speaking to curse at her. Aidriel brushed roughly past as he fled toward the door, fully dressed as she had thought, grabbing the car keys from the table as he went.

The Passers flew after him snarling, their hands reaching out, and though Dreamer called his name, he didn't answer. She heard the door to the stairs at the end of the hall slam open and drift closed, then she hurriedly pulled on her socks and shoes, gathering everything she could carry.

Aidriel took the stairs two and three at a time, using the railing for support and leaping down to the landings. The jumps sent shockwaves of pain up his legs, but at this point, everything hurt. He didn't have time to stop; his life depended on it. He wasn't going to die tonight.

The Passers were pouring densely down the stairway after him, clogging the corridor with ghostly orbs and smoke. Some were hopping over the railing, landing just behind him as he ran. He couldn't recall what floor he had been staying on, but it felt like twenty or thirty by the time he reached the ground floor, the groping hands of the spirits snagging at his shirt. Flinging open the door into the lobby, Aidriel threw himself forward pell-mell, the world a blur around him. He was gripping the car keys so tightly it hurt, but the adrenaline wouldn't let up enough for him to do otherwise.

As he rushed by, Aidriel had an indistinct glimpse of the night clerk looking up from his desk, staring in shock at the sight before him. Aidriel wondered if the other man could see the Passers; either way it would be a strange spectacle.

It was cloudy and moonless outside, and Aidriel was temporarily confused to burst out under

158

the dim lamppost. He couldn't recall immediately where the car was, but when he ran toward it, he saw with a sinking feeling that there was already a handful of Passers standing in and around it. Pitching the keys at them in frustration, Aidriel wheeled to the right and ran blindly out along the street, his attention focused on the horizon. As far as he was concerned, there was nothing around him, and no one. He had to stay away from the town and its people; he had to run until he fell dead in exhaustion or the spirits gave up. Yielding or being caught wasn't an option. He wanted to live tonight.

The bright headlights of a car fell on him from behind, and Aidriel darted across the road quickly enough to not be hit, the sea of Passers just steps behind. He thought he heard the vehicle stall when it passed into the mob of ghosts, but didn't dare glance back. Before him was a trailer-home community, flanked on his left by another road, down which he ran as hard as he could. It was eerie and frightening that he could hear the footfalls of his pursuers, and some of them were screaming out words he couldn't understand.

Up ahead, the headlights of a truck crested a hill, speeding brightly toward him. The horn in the darkness behind the orbs began blaring, and at the last moment, Aidriel turned and darted to the right. The Passers swarmed after him like a cloud of spirit bees, their long claws digging into his back and legs. Aidriel hadn't run far enough to be past the trailer park and had to clear flower pots and scramble over a fence in his flight. He lost his balance and fell on the other side of the fence, instantly getting to his feet and futilely trying to shake off the ghosts. All he could hear was his own labored gasping and the sounds of their nails tearing his shirt and skin.

With a cry of frustration, Aidriel began to run again, throwing himself by force out of their grasp. He dashed past a pond and through the yard of a farmhouse alongside the community, mounting a small hill and dodging around a windmill. On the other side was a large, pitch-black field of young wheat that obstructed his moving legs and slowed him down. Aidriel could see the lights of the main town ahead, and altered his course to run at an angle in hopes of avoiding the streets, keeping on the move and out of the reach of the Passers. A thick grove of trees blocked his path and he had to go out of his way to circle it, forcing through a line of pine trees on the other side.

It was becoming tremendously painful to breathe and run, but he kept on. He ran as if he had been running his entire life, because if he didn't, his life could end right here. His awareness of the ghosts began to become secondary to his conscious effort to suck in air and move his legs, one at a time, in the quickest succession he could muster. The pain within his chest began to overwhelm any pain outside of it, but he ran on.

Eventually Aidriel crossed the expansive field and hurdled a cement curb into the parking lot behind a theatre. High lampposts at intervals made it easier to see where he was, and his steps became more confident. The asphalt caused more shock to his feet and legs, but Aidriel couldn't spare the energy to acknowledge it. He crossed the lot and a strip of grass, entering another huge parking lot in front of the Walmart. There weren't many vehicles

160

on account of the late hour, but he could see a handful of Passers milling about in the smoky yellow light. It didn't take them long to notice the chase and it freshened Aidriel's adrenaline to see them turn to head him off.

Moving with all possible force and drive, Aidriel weaved among the cars without stopping, his arms pumping, the sound of his steps drowned out by those of his chasers. Without hesitation, he dashed right through the Passers that stepped in his way. Their angry talons went through him with the force and pain of bullets, shaving off precious momentum. He stumbled and nearly fell, yet kept on the move, bashing his shoulders against the side mirrors of the cars he passed, continually off balance. One of the vehicles he brushed began to beep furiously in alarm. He dare not look back. He was too afraid and intent on escape to look back.

A Passer stepped into his path; a man with short pale hair and a dagger. It raised the knife at the right moment, and he couldn't stop. The paranormal blade struck him in a perfect blow to the throat and instantly Aidriel's feet flew out from under him. His vision went dark and he choked. He could feel himself falling for the briefest of seconds, then his head struck the pavement with a crack and he blacked out.

Aidriel regained awareness to the feeling of arms all around him, encircling his legs and chest, pulling in two different directions, holding him up at an angle. Blinking away the spots, he realized he was being dragged into a car. Dreamer had the back doors of the vehicle open and her arms around his chest, one hand in a fist and the other gripping her wrist. The Passers were holding onto his legs and were snarling and spitting furiously.

Too dazed to move or speak, Aidriel felt Dreamer release him with one arm to try and block the attacks of the ghosts that had come in through the other side of the car. She yelled out in frustration and swatted at them, then cradled the back of his head briefly. He heard her wiping her hand on her scrubs. When she put her arm around his chest again and resumed pulling, he could see blood all over her fingers.

"Stop it!" she screamed out. "Let go of him, you damned corpses!"

Aidriel could suddenly walk again; his aching legs touched the ground, straining to support him as he stood up, pulling away from Dreamer. He was seeing stars and in terrible pain, but could turn his back on the frothing Passers. He closed the car door on his companion even as she shouted in protest. Sliding into the driver's seat, Aidriel shifted out of park and gunned the already-running engine, screaming out of the parking lot and onto the road. A van slammed on its brakes behind him and blasted its horn. The angry sound halted instantly when the Passers flooded into the street in pursuit.

"Your head is bleeding!" Dreamer said. It took considerable effort for her to pull the other back door closed before climbing into the front seat beside him. "You should let me drive!"

"You'd drive like a girl," he answered, flooring the accelerator and watching the needle slide up the speedometer.

"I drove like a maniac to get to you on time!" she exclaimed.

"You should have driven the other direction!"

162

"Why? What would have happened to you if I had?"

"The point is nothing should happen to *you*." Aidriel's tone softened miserably. "This is *my* problem. I don't want anything to happen to you."

"It's *my* problem now too," Dreamer told him definitively.

"You just watch yourself," Aidriel said after a pause, his capacity to think growing dull. "Keep yourself safe. That's how I want you."

Aidriel felt the hot sticky blood on the back of his head and winced at the accompanying headache that was washing forward through his skull like fire. He pushed past 65mph to 70, then 75; surely there was no way the Passers could catch up. But somehow there was a ghost standing in the middle of the road just over the top of the steep overpass above the turnpike. Aidriel slammed on the brakes, swerving to miss it and nearly colliding with the back end of a car in the oncoming lane. The other horn bleeped at him, and his side of the car ground against the concrete barrier wall with a painful screech. Wrestling the wheel, Aidriel managed to swerve back into the proper lane. He didn't notice how Dreamer was gripping the dash for dear life, only letting go long enough to strap herself in.

Gunning the engine, Aidriel flew right through a stop sign, speeding by a small airport with a white-and-green-flashing beacon. Dreamer stared out the window, then turned in her seat to look back, her head tilting so her hair briefly brushed his shoulder.

"I don't see any," she told him, though both knew that it didn't mean they were out of the woods. The road continued further out into the country, winding around a mostly blind curve with pine trees and dead-ending into another street. Without a thought, Aidriel turned left, following the short stretch back to State Route 108, turning right. He continued to drive in excess of 70mph, unwilling to risk slowing enough for another attack, and turning the brights on to see further down the road, ignoring when other vehicles flashed for him to turn them off.

Dreamer divided her attention between their surroundings and Aidriel. The cut on the back of his head was still hemorrhaging, though less than before, and he was still panting heavily, his limbs shaking with stress and fatigue. Digging through the glove compartment, the phleb found a wad of napkins, which she held to the back of Aidriel's head. She wanted to tell him to breathe easier, to try and relax so his heart would slow down and his cut would clot. She wanted to tell him to pull over somewhere so she could take care of him; so he could stop shaking and rest; so she could take over the wheel. But she couldn't because they weren't far enough away yet.

Aidriel didn't acknowledge her; neither did he take his eyes from the road ahead, barely slowing at another stop sign at a T-intersection. He hesitated, and Dreamer said, "Left."

With a spin of the wheel, he turned and hit the gas again. Dreamer drew her legs up so she was half-kneeling in her chair, her weight leaning against her arm on the back of Aidriel's seat while she kept pressure on his head. Her cell phone buzzed in her pocket, and she instinctively reached for it, but changed her mind and ignored it. She knew that it was one of two people at this hour, and she couldn't speak to either at the moment.

Aidriel allowed the car to slow to the speed limit; his heaving was beginning to calm. It was a small miracle that the automobile and the phone in Dreamer's pocket had not been destroyed by the electromagnetic radiation caused by the Passers. It must be one of those strange occurrences Williams had mentioned about the ghosts doing things just to keep them guessing.

But Dreamer was already guessing. She was only now awake enough to let what had happened sink in, and she still wasn't sure entirely what *had* transpired. She wondered if Aidriel realized that he had very nearly driven off without her. Perhaps he wasn't acting as selfishly as it seemed; he could have thought of protecting her. Maybe that was why he was dressing to leave. He must have somehow known the Passers were coming. But who could blame him for acting only on self-preservation? His life was at risk, not hers.

She was just infinitely glad he had left the keys on the ground beside the car; perhaps it had been intentional. It was fortunate she had caught sight of him crossing the field in the distance, thanks to the ghostly cloud that followed him. Otherwise, she might not have driven in the right direction, and if she hadn't, by now he would be lying in a gory mess in that Walmart parking lot, dead.

CHAPTER 11

"Hey, I have a joke for you."

Dr. St. Cross patiently lowered the medical journal he was reading to look at Todd. They were sitting across the aisle from one another on the cramped little plane, and most of the other passengers were reclined and asleep. The night was dark and starry above the clouds outside the windows, and St. Cross was tired, but Todd was keeping him awake.

"Okay, why are a gorilla's nostrils so big?" asked Todd.

"This can't be going anywhere good," St. Cross replied.

"Because their *fingers* are so big!" Todd exclaimed softly, barely able to contain his amusement and keep his voice low. He broke into a fit of chuckling, and the psychiatrist rolled his eyes.

"That's infantile," St. Cross commented, going back to his reading.

Todd continued to snicker, and the woman beside him lifted her head, opened her sleepy eyes, and gave him a dirty look. Once he had controlled himself, Todd whispered,

"Hey, I wanted to ask you, though—where are we going exactly?"

"Columbus Airport," St. Cross answered, transfixed on his papers. "Then we're taking a charter to the Fulton County Airport in Wauseon."

"Wauseon? Never heard of it."

St. Cross shrugged, and turned the page.

"Nevertheless," he said, "that is our destination."

"Hopefully we're going to a hotel," Todd mumbled, pulling his neck pillow in around his ears and shifting in his chair to make himself comfortable.

"Yes, we are," St. Cross replied with a smile.

Williams and deTarlo had reached the hotel first, and had questioned the night clerk and already left by the time St. Cross and Todd got there. The clerk ran his hand through his spiky hair and twitched nervously.

"I need to make a phone call," he kept saying.

"I just need to ask a few quick questions," St. Cross said in his best shrink voice. To better see him in his wheelchair, the clerk had come around the counter, and was leaning against it as if desperately wanting to be on the other side.

"My boss isn't coming in tonight," he said. "I already called him and he said he'd call the cops, but I don't know what we can tell 'em. There was just a bunch of stuff left behind, and they wrecked the TV and AC/heater unit. It was a good thing I smelled something burning and grabbed the fire extinguisher, 'cause it could'a burned the whole place down!"

"Who did you see?" St. Cross asked, ignoring the drama.

"When? I saw a guy come outta the stairway like a shot, and a bit later a chick with an armload of stuff came outta the elevator. She got in her car and drove off. It took me forever to figure out which room they were in; they left the door open."

"Did you see any Passers?"

"Yeah, I saw a million of 'em chasing after the guy. My computer crashed just before that too, completely fried. Must'a been lightning or a power surge or something."

"You don't know where they went?"

"No, they left hours ago. I heard sirens and called my boss, but I don't know what's going on. You just missed the tall woman in the witch shoes and her son who came in asking about it. Said they came 'cause they tracked a credit card or something. Said they'd pay for everything."

"Did she say her name?"

"No, but she was a Dr. Something. She called her son Chet."

"He's not her son."

"Okay, man, whatever you say. I need to make a phone call. I should really talk to my boss again."

"Just calm down," St. Cross said soothingly. "If something like this upsets you, perhaps you should consider a different profession."

"Yeah, really, right?" piped in Todd. "Weird stuff is always going down in hotels on the night shift. You should be cool as a cucumber." He snickered at his own cleverness.

St. Cross gripped the wheels of his chair, turning it to leave.

"We're not staying here tonight?" asked Todd, disappointed.

The shrink moved a sufficient distance for privacy and took out his cell phone, dialing and smiling in relief when he got an answer. Tilting the receiver away from his mouth, he turned to Todd and said, "Get the car ready. We have to get moving again."

Aidriel finally relinquished the driver's seat to Dreamer when she convinced him to pull over at a Walmart in Elkhart, Indiana, more than two hours after the attack. They parked in the furthest corner of the lot and she ran inside with the credit card from Williams. She knew that Chester's people could see every purchase she made and where, but without access to her own money, she couldn't think of any other way to buy what they needed.

She grabbed a first aid kit, aspirin, a bag of apples, bottles of water, a couple of lightweight khaki jackets, and three plastic five-gallon gas jugs. Aidriel was dizzy and half-asleep when she returned, and once she made sure the cut on the back of his head and a few of the worse scratches on his arms were taken care of, she commandeered the wheel. He swallowed the pain pills on an empty stomach and fell asleep.

Dreamer turned on the GPS and programmed it to guide them to the dead zone in Iowa. The location was a square at the center of four streets out in the middle of nowhere, surrounded, from what she could tell, by nothing but houses and a field.

Her last purchase with the credit card was a full tank of gas in addition to the extra fifteen gallons she put in the trunk, so she wouldn't have to stop again, at least for a while.

As she drove, Dreamer began to feel the anxiety from the night's attack easing a little, and she sneaked a glance from time to time at Aidriel sleeping. At a red light she studied him, taking in his every feature; his uneven but steady breathing, how his eyelashes flickered from time to time. He looked worried, even in his dreams.

Dreamer reached over to take his hand, pulling it up to rest on the lidded compartment between their seats. It wasn't exactly comfortable to have her fingers interlaced with his, if only because she still felt physical contact was premature. But somehow it seemed like she had to do it; like they were stronger holding hands. Aidriel didn't stir, so she didn't let go.

When Dr. Ana deTarlo was working on her *Study of the Psychological Limits of Vasovagel Syncope*, Kara, her Passer, had not spent much time in her company.

At Ana's townhouse, there was a comfortable pair of wicker chairs on her back porch, overlooking a lawn that the landlord kept well-groomed, and a ditch with a trickle of a stream coiling through it. DeTarlo liked to sit in one of the chairs and savor the small victories along the path of her studies. One evening as she was lingering over the last sips of her favorite Cabernet Sauvignon, Kara appeared from nowhere beside the other wicker chair, and slowly sat down.

Kara was much younger than Ana; the girl it had once been was only eighteen when she died

171

and had been a real beauty before the melancholy of its restless purgatory afflicted its features. But it had been a ghost for longer than deTarlo had been alive, and though innocent, it was not naïve.

"I wonder at the ramifications of your study, my friend," Kara mused. "It strikes me as odd that you can call torture, 'research' in the name of psychology."

"It isn't torture," Ana responded in a calm, patronizing tone. She rested her head back against her chair and closed her eyes to enjoy the evening. When something cold brushed her shin, she opened her eyes and was startled to find Kara standing over her.

"Back off!" deTarlo exclaimed, darkly surprised.

"Imagine that tonight, as you sleep, the wires to the outlet by your bed spark and ignite," said the Passer. "You remain blissfully oblivious to the danger even as the nightstand burns, and the bedclothes catch on fire. You only awaken when the flames spread to your nightgown and hair, scorching your skin too quickly for you to react. Imagine as vividly as you can the agony of your crown of fire, burning down your temples and around the back of your scalp, spreading to your forehead, cheeks, ears and neck. Sitting half-upright in your bed, you are overwhelmed with the agony and eventually faint away. Shall I, in the name of research, ask you in your last waking moments what you are feeling? Shall I record how many minutes you could remain conscious and endure the pain? Shall I try to revive you again without putting out the flames, to see if the suffering would keep you in a state of coma, all in the name of psychology?"

Ana was not unmoved to listen to the Passer's description, and barely waited to hear the end of it. Gulping down what was left of her wine and getting swiftly to her feet, she brushed her shoulder through the spirit as she passed.

"Don't be ridiculous," she spat, slamming into the house through the backdoor. "None of my patients are permanently harmed by my study."

"Pain is eternal," Kara told her, drifting through the wall to join her in the kitchen. "Pain lingers in the heart and mind like invisible scars."

"How dramatic."

DeTarlo set her glass down on the sink so harshly, she was surprised it didn't shatter.

"Why have you not asked *me* about pain, my friend?" asked Kara. "*I* know it intimately."

"Is that so? And in what way?"

Kara smiled sadly.

"I have described it to you," the Passer said. "In the last moments, I thought that surely my face and brain were melting. I fell away after less than an agonizing minute. And once I had fainted away, I could not have been revived, if even a person had tried."

Ana furrowed her brow as if she did not believe the spirit.

As if aware of this fact, Kara seemed to relax and release a tense hold of something. Before Ana's eyes, the head of the Passer was engulfed in vague, lightless flames, and its face blurred and melted into horrific features unidentifiable as human. The longer deTarlo stared, unblinking, the more disturbingly bright the echoes of the fiery death wreathed the head of the ghost. Kara burned and beamed with cold white light in edgeless symmetry and lost any semblance of mortality in favor of the unimaginable state of death. Ana thought she was gazing upon a beautiful flaming angel.

"Speak to the Passers," Kara said. "We can tell you with all certainty exactly what the psychological limits of fainting-away pain are."

CHAPTER 12

Dreamer and Aidriel had to get a room at another hotel in East Peoria, Illinois, and were too tired to care that they had to use the *A.S.M.* credit card again. In a daze, they fell into the beds and slept through an uneventful night, though Aidriel awoke several times in a panic. Staring unblinking into the darkness, he was sure the shadows were moving and had to pop pills so he could drift off again.

The next morning, Dreamer was roused to her phone buzzing, and rising to check it, she quietly donned the plain clothes like Aidriel's that she had gathered before they left the last hotel. She put on her shoes and one of the new jackets and slipped silently out the door to return the call.

Aidriel hadn't stirred, but when he got up and found Dreamer gone, he was stunned and slightly worried. He had not changed out of his clothing the night before, but Dreamer had laid out a white T-shirt and his jacket with a pair of black scrubs pants. He got dressed and carefully peeled the blood-caked bandage off the back of his head, gingerly washing his hair at the sink. Finding the injury was well on its way to healing, he went looking for his traveling companion.

She wasn't in the gloomy lobby, or in the little kitchenette area where the complimentary breakfast of bitter coffee and greasy donuts had been set out. Neither was she at the car, or in the parking lot, or back at the room when he double-checked to make sure they hadn't just missed each other in transit.

It was an unpleasant surprise to finally find her in the hotel's pool solarium in the company of Dr. St. Cross, deep in a crucial conversation. As Aidriel approached, Todd spotted him first and got up from one of the tile window benches along the wall of glass panels.

"You're the guy, aren't you?" the nurse asked. "I looked up the video of you on YouTube this morning. Someone at the gas station next to Walmart got the whole thing with their phone of when that Passer nailed you in the throat."

Aidriel was immediately defensive to be greeted in such a way and glared, preparing to respond rudely. St. Cross cut him off by saying his name.

"I'm glad to find you sound, for the most part," the shrink said.

Aidriel looked at Dreamer and narrowed his eyes questioning, wagging his finger back and forth between her and St. Cross.

"What's he doing here?"

"I told him where we were."

"Why?"

"'Cause I thought *he'd* be better than deTarlo."

Aidriel chose to ignore the fact she had made another important action without consulting him.

"You came from Fort Wayne?" he asked the doctor, in no way lowering his defenses.

"Yup," answered Todd. "We went all the way to Columbus, then Wauseon, and back to Indy, then—"

"Who the *hell* are you?" Aidriel demanded of the nurse, whose face flashed surprise.

"I can assure you we had your best interests in mind," St. Cross jumped in to ease the tension.

"Oh sure, it's in my best interest to be left entirely out of all decisions that affect me."

"I'm sorry," apologized Dreamer, "the right time to talk about it never came up. We've been playing phone tag since the Bird Cage."

Aidriel didn't want to say something nasty to her that he would regret, and turned away to quell his anger. His eyes fell on the smooth surface of the water and instantly all emotion melted from his face. He realized he had not been near a pool for twelve years and had never thought of how strong the fear associated with it would be.

"You okay?" Dreamer asked him.

St. Cross shook his head for her to be quiet, but she conveyed without words that she wanted to ask more of Aidriel.

All awareness of the other three people in the room faded as Aidriel stood and stared. The pool was the only thing in the world at the moment, and it was somehow alive and watching him, waiting. The pounding of his pulse rose as it often did, but he was rooted to the spot, mesmerized by the water.

When he was seventeen, Aidriel worked part-time in maintenance at a swanky apartment complex that included a large outdoor pool. On a chilly spring morning like this one, he finished skimming the bugs from the surface of the water and added the chemicals used to maintain it. He had not seen Rubin at all that day, but noticed a shadow in the deep end of the pool as he was leaving. Walking back over to investigate, it seemed to Aidriel that the sun shining on the rippling surface was playing tricks on his eyes. He crouched down for a better look.

The first unfamiliar Passer to ever attack him was a female with long thin arms. It appeared suddenly beneath the water and flew up at him, its eyes and face and mouth a wide white window of rage. It closed its long fingers around his neck and pulled him in headfirst. He experienced the pain of water entering his lungs and never knew if death was by drowning or strangulation. Was there a difference?

Whether by chance or otherwise, the building supervisor was passing through the lobby that looked out over the pool shortly afterward. He didn't notice anything out of the ordinary, but his Passer had stood outside the glass doors and knocked against the panes. It seemed to the supe that the spirit appeared submerged; its surface shimmered with patterned white lines of light through water, and its short dark hair floated out around its head. As he watched, it blew its frigid breath on the glass of the door to fog it, tracing backward letters so the supervisor could read them. POOL. The man was confused but curious, stepping outside to have a look. He saw the teenager at the bottom, already motionless, and yelled out for help, diving in.

"Aidriel," St. Cross interrupted the memory, and his patient tore his gaze from the shimmering water. Dreamer and Todd waited in silent anticipation.

178

"Are you alright?"

Aidriel blinked dully. His recollection of his first death was as fresh as if it were yesterday. That apartment supe hadn't known CPR, though he'd tried it as best he could from what he had seen on television. He'd broken two ribs, but Aidriel started breathing again. He'd been without air for almost five minutes. It'd felt like an eternity.

"What were you thinking just now?" St. Cross asked very softly. "About when you drowned?"

Aidriel couldn't speak, and looked back to the water. He felt the burning in his lungs, the struggle and the panic. He was still drowning. The water was calling him, drawing him toward it. His head was heavy; he was going to fall in and die again.

Dreamer slipped her hand into his to anchor him. Breathing became easier. He locked eyes with her, and she didn't have to say anything.

Aidriel remembered when his vision had come back when he was seventeen, and he saw the supervisor leaning over him, dripping wet and winded.

"You hang in there," the man had said. "I know you already did."

It only now dawned on him why hanging had seemed so right when he chose it to be his means of death. He would never let it be drowning. The noose had not hurt like drowning did.

"You drowned, huh?" said Todd insensitively. "What was that like? Is it painless like they say?"

The pain alone in Aidriel's eyes was an answer.

"Aidriel, it's imperative we get you to the dead zone ASAP," St. Cross said. "I cannot think of any other safe place for you, besides the sky. It seems

179

the only way to leave the Passers behind is to be in a plane or a balloon."

"What about a spaceship?" asked Todd, not realizing how stupid that idea was until several seconds after he had voiced it.

Aidriel wondered what the world outside looked like; if there were legions of Passers waiting for him to make an appearance or an impending storm of them approaching. He let go of Dreamer's hand and moved toward the windows, stepping up onto a tile bench and crouching. It was hazy and moist outside beyond the indistinct green bushes encircling the solarium. He breathed on the glass and touched his finger to the fogged surface, sliding it down slowly to draw a line. His thoughts returned, as they had many times before, to the supervisor's Passer, which had saved his life. He had never seen it and he wondered if he had ever been attacked by it at some later time.

He remembered Rubin, standing over him as he was lying on his back beside the pool, drinking in the delicious air while the supervisor rose up onto his knees to shout at the person who had come in response to his earlier yell to phone for help.

"I'm going to kill you," Rubin had snarled.

"Why?" croaked Aidriel.

"I hate you," the Passer told him. "We all do. I've lost years' worth of opportunities to kill you. Be sure that I will accomplish it, though."

"Aidriel," St. Cross said, once more breaking into his thoughts. "We need to keep moving."

"You said you've been in contact with him, Dreamer?" Aidriel asked without looking back.

"Yes."

"You know each other?" He had an idea of what the answer would be.

"Well…"

"Aidriel, I saw her once for a psych eval for her job at the Coma Center," St. Cross said. "There's no point in lying about it. She reminded me of you, and when I found out she was being considered for employment at the hospital, I put in a word for her. I was actually hoping she might run into you eventually."

"I didn't know that," Dreamer said to the psychiatrist.

"I shouldn't mention it in front of anyone," St. Cross answered, "but your experience with the bear is what reminded me of Aidriel."

"That sounds like an interesting story," commented Todd with a nervous laugh. No one so much as smiled in response.

"What's important," St. Cross said, abruptly changing the subject, "is that we get on the road again as soon as possible."

"You got that right," agreed Todd, adding to Aidriel, "you're a wanted man."

"I was hoping to not have to use the card from Williams again, if that's what you mean," explained Dreamer.

"That is definitely a factor," the shrink replied. "We arrived in Wauseon after deTarlo and Williams had already been there. But there is the issue of the Passers, too."

"We've managed to stay at least several hours ahead of them so far," Dreamer informed him.

"But there're more of them each time, aren't there?" asked St. Cross. "And it's only going to get worse. I don't know if either of you have been following the news but there seems to be a major exodus of the spirits from the other continents traveling in this direction."

Aidriel finally turned from the window, a look of mild dread in his eyes. He sank down so he was sitting on the bench, and began fingering the dog tag still hanging around his neck. DeTarlo had had it altered after his last private conversation with her, and he looked closely at the additional information now engraved on it.

Somehow, hearing that a great number of unstoppable beings were coming to bludgeon him to death did not cause much alarm for Aidriel. He took the news as he would if someone were to tell him that a repair to his car would be more expensive than originally thought. It was bad news indeed, and he was disappointed and upset about it, but it did not warrant even a comment or emotional expression. He felt numb.

"Hey, is he having some kind of episode?" Todd asked curiously. St. Cross bent an eyebrow at the nurse as if to ask, Which of us is the shrink? The nurse shrugged and made a cheeky face, looking for a reaction from Dreamer, but she was ignoring him.

"Good news is," said St. Cross, "we're only about twenty minutes from the Peoria airport, and we can stop in Bartonville for breakfast. I convinced the pilot who took us to Fulton County to take us to Waterloo, Iowa. From there, the dead zone is about an hour's drive away."

"And then what?" asked Aidriel drearily. The doctor shrugged.

"We'll cross that bridge when we get to it."

Aidriel imagined standing alone in the middle of a wide open field, a circle of Passers standing just outside this purported dead zone. In this visual, none of the well-meaning people who had made a mess of his life in the last several weeks were present. They had dropped him off like a package to be delivered and went home to their own lives. He would stand alone to wait out his resolve. It would only be a matter of time before he'd give up and step outside of the safety. How could the dead zone be anything besides another prison? He'd feel smothered; he didn't want to die that way.

"Do you know why you've been singled out?" Dreamer asked him point-blank. Aidriel lowered his head thoughtfully as if he had not heard.

"Are you familiar with the Paradox of Natural Judgment?" St. Cross questioned her.

Frowning in puzzlement, Dreamer replied, "Tracy has mentioned that."

"My Passer has too," added Todd. "I don't think I really know what it means."

"It means that when we die and become Passers, we make someone else's life different than how ours was," Aidriel answered before St. Cross could. "It means the nicest Passers suffered the most, while the mean ones led easy lives."

"But there aren't any mean..." Todd changed his mind about finishing his thought.

"I'm just worried that it might be the reason you suffer so much, Aidriel," said the shrink carefully. His patient got up and walked over until he stood right by the pool, the toes of his shoes lining up with the edge. He gazed down into the water in thought and answered, "The Passers have had ample opportunity to kill me. Each time I died,

I saw a white cloud in the distance like a glow without light. I felt my spirit trapped in my windpipe, trying to force its way out. The horizon turned upside down and all the heat drained out of me so I was very cold. I was just about to let my ghost out when someone brought me back to life, and I was temporarily deaf. Then any pain would suddenly come on like I had been punched."

"What do you think it means?" asked Dreamer, hovering nearby as if worried he would fall into the water.

"It's like…" Aidriel paused in thought, and said without understanding why, "It's like they mean to consume me the moment I become one of them."

He noticed the shocked expression on Dreamer's face, and glancing at St. Cross, noted the shrink appeared disturbed as well.

"Like the dream…," Todd began to interject.

"Dreamer," St. Cross said quickly. "Please get everything from your room so we can leave immediately. I'd like to talk with Aidriel privately, if you please."

Whether it was intentional or not, Dreamer's parents had named her appropriately. In the literal sense of the word, she had vivid dreams nearly every night, except when she succumbed to fitful sleep in times of high stress. But after falling into an anxious doze the dangerous night before, she'd had a brilliant dream until her ringing phone awakened her.

She pondered the sleep-vision while quickly gathering the few belongings she and Aidriel had in the room. Todd had mentioned the first dream that she and Dr. St. Cross and several others had experienced, but she wondered if any of them had had the second vision the night before.

Aidriel's conversation with St. Cross did not take long, and he returned to the room, closing the door behind him. Dreamer was folding clothing at her bed, and sat down on the bedspread, giving Aidriel the attention he appeared to want.

"Do you know how it feels to be completely disconnected?" he put forth, his eyes vacant in thought. "As if you're offline, or unplugged from the network; not getting any signal? Like the whole of the human race is connected with spider silk– thin filaments, but mine has broken so I don't receive any communication at all."

"I'm sorry," Dreamer murmured. "It was selfish of me to make decisions without asking."

"That's not what I'm talking about," Aidriel cut her off quietly. "I just thought maybe you'd get what I mean. Maybe you were a kindred."

Dreamer reflected on his words briefly, but her lips slowly stretched out in a tight line.

"I'm near to that, perhaps," she explained. "But really close, I think. Close enough to experience it."

She held out her hand and moved it as if trying to tear down a string of spider webbing.

"There might something…," Aidriel mused aloud as if he had not heard her.

A quiet moment followed, and an outside observer might have thought the conversation had drifted into nothing because it didn't concern the two. Aidriel leaned against the wall and glanced around as if unsure what to do next. His thoughts escaped for a moment to superficial imaginings of the future. He fancied he'd buy fruit from roadside vendors and would sweep the cobwebs from the corners of the kitchen ceiling when he got home. Dreamer would shake rugs and the tablecloth off the edge of the porch, and leave the door open to let the breeze in. Spring would find them the way it came to everyone else living normal lives, and for a time they'd be too distracted to think of the ghosts of their pasts. He would get the blender down from his cupboard for Dreamer, because she was shorter than he, and couldn't reach it. She'd make an orange cream milkshake and would pour it into tall glasses with straws, wiping the drippings from the counter before tasting it. She would make him laugh, and he would cheer her up again when he made her cry.

"Things could be normal," he mused. They could be so peaceful together.

Aidriel forgot that Dreamer wasn't imagining the same things he was, and looked at her to witness her agreement. But she didn't understand; her thoughts were still in the present. All his plans vanished in an instant, and so suddenly it pained him. He glanced at her accusingly, because she wasn't receiving his signals.

Dreamer sadly lowered her eyes, choosing her words before speaking.

"How long have you been a target to the Passers, even before the attacks?"

Aidriel put his hand thoughtfully over his mouth.

"Is this another session?" His voice sounded muffled behind it. He didn't answer her question.

186

Dreamer finished folding the shirt she had let rest on her lap, making him wait for her to speak.

"I dreamt of you last night," she told him, laying it aside. "This is the second about you. I could see your pulse like purple lightning, coursing out from your heart. It flashed in the dark quickly at first, but slowed down. You were tired—*are* tired."

Even as she talked, Aidriel sank down on his bed to listen.

"You've got…," Dreamer continued hesitantly, suddenly self-conscious. "You've got the weight of the world on your shoulders."

Aidriel sighed deeply in agreement.

"I want to disconnect," stated Dreamer. "I want to be on *your* network."

"It's a lonely signal," Aidriel responded, half-smiling bitterly at the strangeness of his words.

"I'll respond to it."

Aidriel repeated his partial grin and shook his head.

"I realize that dreams are not real," she said, "but since I was a little girl I've been having nightmares about bears. They *feel* very real, and have caused a subconscious hurt by association. Your hurt is much worse, and deep-seated, but I kind of know what that pain looks like, so I can see it."

"So it doesn't even matter what happens," Aidriel muttered. "The damage has long since been done."

"That sounds so hopeless. Regardless of what's happened to you, what do you *need*? What could…I don't know, save you?"

"I need reprieve. I need peace and normalcy. I need air. I need help. I need to *breathe*."

187

Dreamer got up without him noticing.

Aidriel lapsed into his memories; it was easier than imagining the future. He recalled awakening in agitation the night he was attacked after Dreamer had resisted his advances. He had sat in the darkness, peering at the outline of her asleep in her bed, straining to hear her silent breathing. He sensed the Passers were coming, but he knew he couldn't wake her up. Though distracted by his thoughts, he had dressed swiftly and silently, sitting on his bed to put on his shoes. He had paused, dreading having to leave without her. It was safer for her that way, but then her fears would be right; he would be abandoning her. He'd envisioned awakening her and dragging her through thick and thin, but had been unable to do it. The hesitation of wondering if she would stir if he touched her or kissed her goodbye had cost Aidriel in the end; he'd lingered too long and was taken by surprise by the aggressive swarm. Yet the assault had roused Dreamer; the question of whether to leave without her had not been one he'd had to answer. Just remembering how he was intending to leave her ashamed him. It was damaging to realize one had been abandoned.

Aidriel saw in his memory how his dad's truck looked that last time he saw it, driving away down the road, taking the curve and disappearing. He remembered vividly the sense of being alone, even though he technically hadn't been. Sometimes it was terrible to be alone.

The bed shifted beneath him, and he came back to the present, finding himself staring at Dreamer, who had sat down across from him. Her face was calm, her light eyes fixed on his steadily.

188

His senses recalled the last real-life moment of comfort for him; the surreal rocking, the weightless drifting of his body hanging from the noose.

His equilibrium was unmoored and his thoughts were in an orderly confusion, unable to focus on exclusively what had happened, what was happening, or what could happen, without skipping intermittently among them. He didn't like the future; there had never been a reason to hope for any change. But there were more options than he had ever let himself picture. Dreamer was trying to ground him and connect with him without words. She would have succeeded, perhaps, had Todd not pounded on the door, calling that it was time to get going.

Chester Williams sat on the top step of the rolling stairway against the side of his plane, his hand gripping his computer touchpad between his knees, on which he tapped with a stylus. He had his Bluetooth device in his ear, and for hours had gone from one conversation to another, reiterating the same information and hearing the same reports. In the distance, he could see the beginning of a thunderstorm shaking the tops of the trees. The wind fluttered the hem of his coat, but he was too focused on the information he was streaming on the handheld screen to notice.

Jack Stickney was on the other end of the line and was sparing no harshness toward the Passerist.

"I've been trying to reach you for almost three hours," was the first thing Jack had said grumpily, and out of pure exhaustion, Williams didn't bother to tell him that pretty much everyone with any of his private numbers had been calling him.

"I've received all the recent reports about the protests," Chester said. "I know about the fire in Denver, and about the migration in Europe and Asia, and about the riot in Gettysburg and about the end of the credit card trail in Bartonville, Illinois. I talked with Fagin. No, I'm not shirking my responsibilities, and if I was, it's none of your freaking business."

"Then lucky for you, I'm not calling about any of those things," Jack answered.

"Shock me."

"I got a call from St. Cross the other day, and he was really pissed about you interfering with his patient."

"Has he called back, or did he leave a number?"

"No, do you want me to get a hold of him?"

"If you can. He might actually know where *his* patient is."

"Nothing came up in Bartonville?"

"I said that, didn't I? No, they haven't used the card since, and they left their car at the airport."

"So they are heading toward Iowa."

"You're a genius," Chester said nastily.

"Where are you?"

"Des Moines. Had that thing in Farrar I was supposed to go to. A car's on the way, then we're heading to the dead zone."

"Dr. deTarlo going with you?"

Williams just groaned.

"What about the protest there?" asked Stickney.

"If I ever finish with the endless phone calls, we'll be heading there next."

"Boy, are you a masochist or what?"

"It's called accountability," Chester responded snippily. "I don't have the time to chase some random guy around just because he has a problem with Passers. *A.S.M.* won't run itself."

"Actually, it will."

In a snit, Williams pressed the button on his ear device to hang up, assuming the insolent intern would call back if he got anything from or about St. Cross. The clouds were drawing nearer and the wind was picking up, but the temperature hadn't dropped yet, and the rain still wasn't falling.

He wearily answered the next call-waiting.

"Finally," deTarlo sighed. "You've got three lines and all of them were busy at once. I was lucky it finally rang through."

"Oh, for the days of face-to-face conversations," Chester responded sarcastically.

She'd left hours ago with his assistant to head northwest to little Farrar, Iowa, with its haunted school house to sit in on a Passerist meeting there, which Williams had wanted to attend but couldn't find the time for. The psychologist had made some vague mention of accumulating expert commentary, but Chester had just been glad to be rid of her for a little while.

"You're not the only one with things to do," she chided him. "I know how much you enjoy my company, but—"

"Are you bugging me for a reason?"

"Rod and Kara were here earlier. They're on their way to meet you at the airport."

"How long?" Chester asked, looking at his watch.

"Forty-five minutes if we're lucky. Rod has something to tell you."

"Why didn't it tell *you*?"

"You'll have to ask it."

"Anything else?"

"No. We're heading back. I'll see you—"

The Passerist pressed the button on the Bluetooth again, sighed, and said, "Chester Williams."

When Rod and Kara arrived at the airstrip, Williams had retreated into the plane at the arrival of the storm, and was sitting by the window, watching for them. They stood at the bottom of the steps and didn't ascend them, so the Passerist came to the door, holding a hand up to shield his face from the rain.

"We're going to the dead zone, my friend," Rod told him, unaffected by the falling water. "Everyone is. He's on his way there."

"I already know that," Chester answered.

"Did you know that I was there the first time he was attacked?" asked Rod.

"At the Bird Cage? Yes, I know."

"No. The *first* time."

"Twelve years ago? Before you came to me?"

"Yes, when his journey was just beginning. I sounded the silent warning."

"No, I didn't know that. Why didn't you say…?"

192

"It does not affect the present. I withhold no secrets of the past from you, and will speak now of the near future. Are you listening to me?"

"Yes…" Chester was slightly unbalanced. Before his eyes, the dimly human resemblances of the two Passers were changing; Kara's head and shoulders were wreathed in an immense, bright colorless flame impervious to the rain, and Rod's hair drifted in an unseen flood, the surface of the spirit's skin and garments marbling with wavy lines of translucent light.

"You'll send the girl a message," Rod told him. "You'll tell her to tell him to stop being afraid. He must no longer be afraid."

"You'll tell her to tell him to stop running," added Kara. "He mustn't run another step."

"He's going to die," said Rod, raising its eyes upward as its clothing floated out in the same submerged manner as its hair. "Under the sky, he'll give up the ghost. Today; this afternoon."

"How?" Chester asked, squinting through the rain.

Rod and Kara answered at the same time:
"Rubin."

CHAPTER 13

The waitress topped off Aidriel's coffee and checked to see if Dreamer needed more. The two were perched on the stools at the bar of a little diner within walking distance of the Waterloo airport. The flight had thankfully been short and safe, but Aidriel was downing more and more painkillers, and still couldn't seem to take the edge off. He was perpetually achy and groggy, and had been on the side of irritable since St. Cross showed up.

Dreamer was often sore herself—the residual effects of the ambulance crash—but she felt more alert by ignoring the pain and remaining off the analgesics. She rested one hand on the bar, swiveling her stool back and forth, her eyes on the empty sidewalk outside. There was no one else in the diner but an elderly couple eating pancakes, their Passers nowhere in sight.

Aidriel leaned against the bar wearily, staring down into his steaming brew and sulking. What he was upset about at present, Dreamer wasn't sure, but he had been less than civil with her, so she didn't bother to ask. Depending on how fresh of a dose of pills he was on or how acute his discomfort, he was warm and inclusive of her or cold and distant. The last couple hours he had been ignoring anything said to him and remaining lost in thought.

St. Cross and Todd had separated from them at the airport; where they had gone was anyone's guess. Probably to get another rental car. The days seemed to be long progressions of driving, flying, and procuring transport. At least they were in Iowa now.

Dreamer's cell phone buzzed in her pocket, and expecting to hear from the shrink, she took it out. Surprisingly, Chester Williams had texted her. He had begun trying to call or reach her by text right after she lost them on the expressway. But he'd given up on contact some time ago. She thought that he'd finally gotten the hint that she was intentionally ignoring him. This was an urgent message.

Aidriel was nursing his coffee and paying her no attention, so she got up to check the text outside where the signal would be better, in case she felt the need to call Williams. The little bell above the door rang as she went out; she chose a spot at the corner of the storefront by an unkempt shrub.

The message read: URGENT: TELL AA TO STOP FEAR & RUNNING.

Dreamer wasn't clear on the meaning at first, and would have simply blown it off as a demand to return to deTarlo's care, based on the "running" part. But why had he told her to tell Aidriel to stop being afraid? Had the Passerist realized something about the spirits that could help Aidriel?

The phleb hesitated, her finger over the button to dial the callback number. She was very interested in finding out what Chester meant, but at the same time was worried he could somehow figure out where she was if she called him. She knew that it was possible to track cell phones down to a ten-foot area, but reasoned that since her mobile that been on all this time, they could have already tracked her if they wanted to.

She pressed dial, crossing her free arm across her chest to support the hand holding the phone, and braced herself for whatever the conversation would entail.

In the diner, Aidriel continued to lean against the counter tiredly, rubbing his eye with the heel of his hand, and remaining oblivious to his surroundings. A sudden jolt of pain in the pit of his stomach startled him, and though he waited, he didn't hear any ringing. He looked up and toward the door to see if Dreamer was coming back in, but she wasn't. There was, however, a female Passer standing just inside the glass, staring at him.

It had long wavy dark hair and a young face. Aidriel recognized it; it was the strangling ghost that had been present at the attack in the Bird Cage. For some reason, it was standing still and waiting, not launching at him. His heart pounding, Aidriel watched it.

Behind the Passer, Dreamer opened the door and came back in, her eyes lowered on the phone in her hand. As she put the cell into her pocket and looked up, she spotted the staring spirit and stepped swiftly between it and Aidriel.

"Tracy!" she exclaimed nervously. "Where have you been? What're you doing here?"

"Wandering," Tracy answered flatly. It lifted its ashen hand and pointed a long nail at Aidriel accusingly. Dreamer looked swiftly at him over her shoulder.

"Don't be scared of it," she said. "I just talked with Williams, and he said that you might have a better chance of safety if you don't act afraid."

Aidriel slid off his stool nonchalantly, adjusting the collar of the gray wool coat he had switched to in the airport. The jacket Dreamer had given him wasn't warm enough.

"Is this your Passer?" he asked Dreamer. It took a certain resolve to follow her advice and not run like a rabbit as he was accustomed to doing.

Dreamer swallowed, keeping her eyes on Tracy, muttering an affirmative.

"What're you after?" Aidriel asked the Passer. It continued to point at his face.

"Yeah, but why?" demanded Dreamer. "The ghosts didn't harass you when you were alive! What is it? You aren't a vengeful Passer!"

Tracy smiled slightly, stretching its arm as far forward as it could, still pointing. Aidriel glanced at the door behind the ghost and wondered if he could get past it and Dreamer without suffering much injury. He didn't know if there was a back door. It had been stupid to come in here in the first place. But he remained still, stuffing his hands apprehensively into his pockets and deliberately telling himself to be calm. Williams was a Passerist; surely he knew more than the average person did about the spirits. He would probably not give advice for Aidriel to do something dangerous intentionally. After all, Chester had partnered with deTarlo for their stupid study, which as of yet was not completed.

Tracy took a threatening step forward, its face contorting in wrath. It seemed to Aidriel to be stalling, and he wondered if it was waiting for the backup of other Passers. He kept his attention on the ghost while Dreamer took out her phone and looked at the display, pressing a few buttons.

"St. Cross and Todd are waiting for us at the airport," she said without turning.

Aidriel glanced again at the door. They were only a couple of blocks from the airport gate. They could make a run for it.

Tracy advanced another step, jabbing its arm forward threateningly. Dreamer was becoming upset, and took a swing at Tracy's hand, snapping, "Knock it off!"

Aidriel turned, unfolding a few of the dollar bills that St. Cross had given him to lay on the counter before the gawking waitress. He forced himself to remain cool as he pocketed the rest of the money. Then with a snap of movement, he darted past Dreamer, catching her by the arm and dragging her out the door.

They fled down the sidewalk toward the airport, running as hard as they could, but not risking a glance back until they were dashing up the long drive toward the terminal. Tracy was nowhere in sight behind them, and Aidriel felt as if he had dodged a bullet.

The city hall of Des Moines, Iowa, was a majestic structure built in the three-story Beaux-Arts style—long and rectangular, accented with faux pillars and made of cream-colored granite. It was fronted by gardens and a wide staircase leading down into a field that ended at the Des Moines River. Camped out all over the pristine front lawn were protesters. Their efforts dampened by the rain, clusters of people stood miserably under umbrellas or stretched blankets over their heads to try and stay dry, their posters and signs sagging in the downpour.

Chester Williams sat in the front passenger seat of his car, parked along the side of Locust Street, a road that ran at a right angle to City Hall. Chester had told his assistant to pull over so he could gauge the scene before entering it. DeTarlo lurked behind him, her presence intense as if she could guess that he had spoken with Dreamer and hadn't told her. She was, however, patiently silent, dividing her glances between Williams and the soggy picketers. Nothing seemed to be happening.

Chester was a very hands-on manager. He was young and vital enough to not wish for a simple overseer position. He micromanaged *A.S.M.*, which annoyed some and inspired awe in others. It took effort for him to ignore the constant requests for guidance in petty tasks by his employees. Some of them were too dependent on him, he felt, and he relied on Fagin, his close friend and the director of *A.S.M.* in his absence, to handle the things that he couldn't. The fact that Fagin had had very little contact with him since his departure only cemented Chester's trust that the other man was busy taking care of the organization and didn't have the time or need to ask for help.

When the private orderlies, doctors, and other temporary staff members were assembled for the trip to Kelly Road, Williams had personally seen to their "orientation." Chester liked to pick and choose which tasks he wanted to handle himself and which he passed off to others. It was the privilege of leadership, and the only way to fulfill the need he

200

was born with to be moving and doing things his own way.

That was why he was sitting here in Des Moines; him, Chester Williams, a leading voice in Passerism and the head of the American Sentience Movement. He went whenever he could, if it mattered to him, which it had not where the Farrar meeting was concerned. But he hated having to send a representative to anything he had a specific outlook on, because they invariably made things worse and never handled it how he would. It was Chester's opinion that if there were three or four identical copies of him, these protests would all be taken care of by now.

"What're we waiting for?" deTarlo breathed, as if afraid of breaking a spell.

"I'm looking," Chester responded. "I don't rush in blindly."

"Ah." Her tone of voice left it ambiguous whether she was agreeing genuinely or ironically.

Chester signaled to his assistant, who started the car and drove up to East 1st Street and turned left, parking in the lot in the rear of the building. Getting out, Williams took a deep breath and entered the hall, deTarlo and the assistant following several steps behind.

The Passerist did not require an introduction, and was almost immediately ushered into the mayor's office. His assistant and deTarlo sat down on a bench in the lobby area to wait.

Ana watched the comings and goings of the City Hall, observing in particular the Passers. Most of them ignored her presence completely, though they glanced around and at one another often, as if waiting for something. She fixed her attention on

201

the assistant, who distractedly tapped at his laptop. He sensed she was staring at him, and looked up.

"Any word?" she asked. "On the two of them?"

Williams's assistant shook his head apologetically, and Ana sulked.

In a few minutes, Chester returned looking exasperated.

"Sometimes I think I'm the only non-idiot left in this country," he exclaimed. "These people think they can protest the Passers, but never once think that maybe they have just as much influence over the spirits as the rest of us!"

The assistant looked around as if trying to figure out how to respond, and Chester moved in agitation for a few moments, shifting his feet and resting one hand on the wall beside the bench while gesturing with the other.

"The mayor's completely ineffectual, of course," he continued. "*I'll* have to try to talk to these nutjobs."

Before deTarlo could get out the words she clearly wanted to say, Williams marched across the lobby, past a secretary's desk, down a hall of offices, into a second lobby area, down another long hall with closed doors and out the front corridor of the building.

The rain was letting up as the Passerist stepped onto the stone veranda and crossed to position himself at the top of the stairs. The protesters began to stand if they were sitting, approach if they were standing, and talk if they weren't all ready. Chester didn't appear to know or care if they were aware of who he was, but held up a hand for silence. A reluctant hush fell over the crowd.

"Everyone has a right to their opinion," Williams started, projecting his voice in an experienced fashion. "We hear and understand your viewpoint; that the Passers are not good for public welfare. That they may be a danger, or are making us dependent, even that they are simply unnatural. You may be right; it hasn't been long enough since the Sentience to say with any certainty. But the way you go about making your opinion known is not going to get you results."

"So you're not going to do anything, then?" someone shouted from the crowd.

"No, I'm saying," Chester responded with evident patience, "that none of us have any more control over the Passers than anyone else. Just because you demand of the government for the ghosts to leave us alone doesn't mean anything can be done for you. Should the government choose to grant your demands, and tell the Passers to pass on by, do you think the spirits would listen? Have you tried speaking to your own Passer companions and asking them to leave?"

"Do you think we're stupid?" a protester shouted.

"Yes, actually," Williams countered too quietly to be heard.

"We tried that!" another voice screeched. "It didn't work! The Passers are haunting our streets and homes and businesses like we live in a graveyard!"

Others began shouting and jeering in agreement.

"We can't force them to go!" Chester yelled above the noise. "They aren't physical entities! They won't go unless they choose to!"

203

"Who is this moron?" a loud man near the front demanded to know. "I want to talk to someone who isn't useless!"

"Yeah, who are you, anyway?" people began calling in agreement.

"I can't believe these idiots," Chester said just loudly enough for deTarlo and his assistant to hear him. "The same bullshit everywhere I go."

The protesters were becoming more animated and upset, and deTarlo started to back up, leaving Williams and his meek assistant at the stairs. Chester was feeding off the anger of the crowd and was becoming upset himself, but unexpectedly recalled what Rod had said to him when they were discussing Aidriel. His Passer had advised him to walk away when "they" became violent. Chester had simply assumed since then that the warning was about Passers; he hadn't figured it could be about this unruly group of soggy picketers.

It was not Williams's nature to walk away from a fight, no matter the odds, but he knew that Rod had watched his back on numerous occasions, and should be trusted.

The Passerist was reluctantly turning to leave when a bottle sailed by him and shattered on the stone veranda of the City Hall. If he'd still been addressing the crowd, it would have hit him in the face. Instantly enraged, Chester turned and was about ready to fly down the stairs when his assistant caught him by the arm and pulled him back.

It took only the few seconds while Williams tried to extricate himself from his assistant for the Passerist to notice the moving fog in the distance to his left, southwest on the Des Moines River.

Ceasing his struggle, Chester felt his wrath evaporate, replaced with curiosity. Of course he knew exactly what he was looking at, but he was confused by the sight.

Startled and frightened out of their bloodlust by Williams's strange reaction, the protesters began hushing and turning, following his gaze out along the river's width. In a minute or two, a silence had fallen over the group as they all stood and stared at the moving mass of Passers. Their hatred for the spirits aside, the crowd was too befuddled to react. A visible migration of the spirits, like Tosya had described to Chester, was clearly taking place. Glancing to his right, Williams saw that more clutches of the ghosts could be seen crossing the river to the north, all of them heading northeast. It was curious none of them were passing near enough to the City Hall to be clearly seen.

"What's going on?" someone called out, afraid.

"My sister in Chicago called me about this!" a woman loudly answered. "She said the Passers are all just walking away without a word! Maybe our protests are having an effect!"

The crowd began murmuring and buzzing in conversation, but Chester just shook his head.

"Think that if you like," he muttered.

His assistant glanced at his watch and said something about moving on. DeTarlo turned immediately to leave, but Williams was more interested in observing the fascinating migration of the Passers. He wished Rod was here to shed some light on what was happening.

"We'll see more on the road, I'm sure," Ana said. "Let's go, Chet."

Williams ignored her, and she and the assistant were forced to wait several minutes until Chester felt he had seen enough. The mob, in the meantime, had fully embraced the idea that the Passers were leaving as they had demanded, and became animated again, despite a stiff wind blowing across their damp clothing. Raising their voices in victory chants of sorts, the protesters yelled after Chester and his companions as they left.

"So much for that, Mr. Expert Guy!" taunted the loudmouthed man in the front of the crowd. "Guess you're an expert at sticking your foot in your mouth!"

"I'd like to be an expert at sticking it in *your* mouth," Chester retorted under his breath as the door closed behind him, and he and the others began to cross the building again to get to the car.

Sliding into the front passenger seat, Williams immediately put his Bluetooth into his ear to make phone calls and tuned out deTarlo's condescending questions. Ana shrugged him off and with relish began to write on her clipboard. After a while, she paused to reread a line of text with satisfaction, mouthing the word *remarkable* and smiling to herself.

The drive from Des Moines to Wellsburg took Williams's assistant more than two and a half hours with the traffic jams the Passer migration was causing. The three in the car were relieved to finally reach the town where it seemed everyone in the country was going.

DeTarlo leaned back to rest her eyes and, in her own little world, imagined the praises her peers would be singing once she published her report. Chester was poking at his tablet in the front seat, oblivious to his assistant's frustration at driving. The police car escorting them through Wellsburg had its lights flashing, but it's siren off as it threaded its way through the roadblocks and crowds in the avenues. They pulled into the driveway of a house on one of the streets that formed the intersection where the dead zone was. The owners of the house were standing on their porch, one talking to a police officer while another was videotaping the migration of Passers. It was mostly sunny; the rain seemed to have missed Wellsburg.

Williams's assistant turned off the car and slumped back in his seat with a sigh. Hesitating for a moment, he unstrapped and got out to consult with the cops. Chester continued to tap a while longer, then set aside his tablet. He took in the sight outside the car with a look of dread on his face. It was expected by everyone that since he was an expert, he'd know exactly what was going on. The stinging of his pride was still fresh from the protest; as if it were somehow his fault that Passers existed.

"You alright, Chet?" deTarlo asked in a shrink voice. "You need some time to regroup?"

Williams ignored her, staring intently out the window.

"We haven't had time for personal conversation, have we?" Ana said. "It's all the project or business correspondences, it seems."

"I have responsibilities."

"How's Olivia, by the way?" deTarlo asked, sitting forward so she could see his face better.

"You've had a long engagement, if I'm not mistaken. Have you made her Mrs. Williams yet?"

"Shut up."

"And what about the little one? Bonnie's her name, right?"

"Her name is Argentina," Chester responded hostilely.

He didn't say that only people in his closest circle could call her Bonnie. Argentina was a mouthful, and was a reminder of how her mother wasn't in her right mind when she named her. Those who knew her called her Bonnie because of her large dark eyes and thick eyelashes, a gift from her mother, who was of either Indian or Pakistani descent.

"How old is she now?" asked deTarlo, ignoring his tone. "Five?"

"Four. It's none of your business."

The psychologist sat back again and smiled smugly.

"I've known her since birth too, you know," she said.

DeTarlo used to be Bonnie's mother's shrink, before the mentally unsound woman found herself broke and arrested for skimming when Williams gave her a job. While she was in prison, she left her daughter in Chester's care because she knew he was financially stable. He wasn't the father, but Bonnie's real dad had disappeared before she was even born. Williams had resisted her at first, but Olivia, who was still his girlfriend and not his fiancée yet, had fallen in love with the little girl and insisted she would look after her.

"Is she in kindergarten?" deTarlo pressed. "She was a creative little one, if I remember. Used to draw pictures on the floor of my office. Does she have a Passer yet?"

Chester shifted uncomfortably and kept his gaze out the window. He did not like that Ana knew things about his personal life, but how could she not? She had met him as a teenager through Bonnie's mother, long before the child was born, and through him, she became acquainted with his divorcé father. Russell Williams was almost ten years older than Ana, but they had spent six years in a relationship before it fizzled out into a friendship with lasting strings attached on both sides.

In that time, she'd learned about and fawned over Chester's unique ability to see all Passers. It was thanks to her insistence and financial support that he went to Bennington College for Public Action and Political and Social Sciences, and studied paranormal phenomena in the Princeton Engineering Anomalies Research program before it was closed down. He was bright and gifted; it didn't take him long to acquire multiple degrees. But having a title and being a respected expert were two different things that were difficult to bring together for someone so young and inexperienced.

DeTarlo had not been satisfied. She would sometimes have speaking appearances on a radio station during an "Ask the Doctor"–type show, and had convinced one of the DJs to interview Williams. That was only the start of the many debts she called in to get his name out and his face recognized by the public, much of it without consulting him first. But how could he complain when he was benefiting from it?

"Doesn't she miss you while you're gone?" deTarlo asked, meaning Bonnie. "I think if I had a session with her, we'd find out she has issues with separation."

Chester bristled. It was never his intention to separate himself from Bonnie like her mother had after she got out of jail. He hadn't seen the woman in more than a year, but he hoped he never would again. It was obvious in retrospect that she had insisted he legally take custody of the child while she was in prison because she wanted Bonnie to be taken care of for life. So when Williams realized he had a permanent ward, he had stopped insisting the little girl call him by his name. He was Bonnie's daddy now, and would remain so. There was no way that her mother could take her back, even if she wanted to. Liv was her new mommy. Both of them knew he wouldn't and wasn't trying to remain detached from them. But his previous life and previous attachments still demanded his attention.

"I seem to recall," he said sharply to deTarlo, "that I was in *Denver* with my family when my dad's ex-floozy demanded I come to Fort Wayne."

"As if this trip is the only one you've taken recently," responded Ana. "With a respected position like yours, you have hardly any free time to spend with your loved ones."

Chester instinctively prepared to argue that it was ironic she was the one saying that, since she had so drastically changed the course of his life. If he hadn't initiated the American Sentience Movement, he might not have been wealthy enough for Bonnie's mother to choose to leave her to him, and he would not have met Olivia.

210

As if reading his mind, DeTarlo nodded and smoothing her skirt and opening the door of the car to get out. Chester got out too, surveying the area, feeling the dread of preparing to plunge into another difficult situation.

"Chet," said Ana, though he didn't turn. "You're only here because of me."

As he strode toward the police officers congregating on the porch of the house, his hands in the pockets of his sport coat, Williams looked back at her and said, "You're exactly right."

Despite his discourteous actions, it was not at all the case that Aidriel wanted nothing to do with Dreamer. Sitting side by side in the back of the car that Todd was driving like a maniac through strangely docile Passers clogging the streets of Waterloo, Aidriel felt there was something he needed to tell her. She was staring thoughtfully at the display of her phone, though she didn't press any buttons, and he knew they had a ride of at least an hour ahead of them. But he had a heavy sense of something he needed to get out in the open; he just wasn't entirely sure what it was.

"Dreamer," Aidriel said softly, hoping to go unheard by the two men in the front seats. "I'm sorry about what happened at the hotel. I didn't want to upset you, but I'm not sorry for what I did."

She looked up and smiled bashfully.

"It's nothing to do with me," she said. "I can't imagine anything I've experienced compares to what *you* have."

"That's been building for years. I don't want to talk about that; what happened is totally unrelated. I still want to pick up where we kind of were when we left off."

"Meaning?"

He could tell by the sly grin on her face she was waiting to hear something in particular.

"After this, do you want to…?" Aidriel realized Todd and St. Cross were watching him in the rearview mirror, obviously considering the conversation public enough to listen in on it.

Leaning over with the intent to speak closely in her ear, Aidriel got an indistinct hint of her shampoo and smiled. He put his nose into her hair to smell it, and this time she didn't pull away. He could feel her chuckle soundlessly.

"Well?" demanded Todd, straining to see in the mirror. "What'd she say? What'd you say, Dreamer? You guys gonna go out?"

"Todd, watch the road," St. Cross ordered, turning his attention back to an open file on his lap. "Mind your own business."

"Hey, it *is* my business!" Todd insisted. "He asks her out in my car, it's my business."

"I say yes, Todd," Dreamer said, adding softly, "though it isn't your business."

"Now watch the road," St. Cross said, pointing forward. "You're making me nervous."

Aidriel sat up straight again, clasping his fingers around the top of Dreamer's half-closed left hand at her side. It felt instinctual, like how he had imagined them when he was at the first hotel. He gazed at her face until he felt he was staring, then turned his head to watch her out of the corner of his eye. Her cheeks were pleasantly flushed; she knew he was observing her.

"When it's over," she said with a knowing smile.

Aidriel looked out the window at the passing city and thought that perhaps there was a glimmer of hope on the horizon. As if reading his mind, St. Cross said, "Things are not fine and dandy yet. The crap could hit the fan all at once in the next hour, and almost certainly will." He was staring grimly out the windshield.

Aidriel noticed that though they had been encountering flocks of Passers since they left the airport and none had as of yet attacked, they appeared to becoming more and more numerous. There had to be hundreds of them by now, all walking in the same direction, their attention straight ahead, oblivious of everyone around them, even him. Pedestrians on the street would try unsuccessfully to ask them questions, or would stand aside and watch in awed curiosity. Todd even drove past a news crew filming the strange migration.

Releasing Dreamer's hand, Aidriel gripped the door handle, his eyes glued on the sight. The crowd of spirits was becoming denser. Where had they come from so suddenly? The familiar physical warnings of an attack began stirring, but he forced himself to remain calm. He could hear the rate of his breathing increase and it was making him light-headed.

"Wow, this is all because of Aid?" asked Todd, watching the flood of spirits crossing the street in his path.

"Look at the cars, though," said Dreamer. "No electromagnetic disturbance. That's strange."

The others sat quietly, observing that what she said was true, and it puzzled them.

"Perhaps the electromagnetism is only when the Passers are upset," commented St. Cross. "Think about it; Passers exist in our day-to-day lives without disrupting our electronics. Perhaps it's only when they're upset, and since so many have been congregating around Aidriel, they create a strong enough field to destroy things."

Aidriel reached up subconsciously and laid his fingers against the window, tracing an invisible line down the glass. He looked to the faces of the ghosts they passed, but all the translucent facades were blank and facing their destination.

"There's no way I'm going to get to that dead zone," he whispered.

"Yes you are," Dreamer responded resolutely. "If we have to drag you into it against a million Passers, we'll do it."

"Who's 'we'?" asked Todd. "Doc's in a wheelchair and you're a girl."

"So?" she demanded. "*You* haven't seen what'll happen if we don't."

"No one's going to drag me," said Aidriel.

"Well, if we have to," Todd talked over him, "I hope Williams and his goons are actually there like we think, so they can help me."

"You sexist twit," Dreamer growled under her breath.

Aidriel had nearly forgotten about Williams and deTarlo, and realized they were most likely already at the dead zone or on their way.

It was alarming to think that the worst, most challenging race of his life could be only an hour away. He dreaded the ending of this journey, and

214

could sense that the closer they came to it, the others feared it also. That Todd had pointed out the others' general disability to help him made him all the more anxious. When it came down to it, when he would step out of the car and run for the small area—wherever it was—where he could be safe, no one was going to help him. His own two aching legs would have to carry him, and if they failed, he wouldn't reach it at all.

The day Aidriel arrived, barely alive, at the emergency room had been hazy and damp, and he had awakened late with the feeling that something was on the verge of happening. It took effort to reluctantly drag himself out of bed. His money was almost gone, and it was difficult to function. There was no point in looking for another job.

Standing at the small window in the main room of his apartment, he could see the early-spring wind blowing violently through the tree growing in the middle of the sidewalk. It was storm-perfect weather, but the clouds held back the rain. The dancing leaves were strikingly beautiful, and the coffee Aidriel had brewed tasted just right. It was the last of the cream; there wasn't enough money for more. It was the day, then. The day he had been waiting years for.

Listening to the whistling of the wind against the building, Aidriel had taken his time knotting the rope. He watched the emergence of the noose, and felt like he was creating something. It had been so long since he made something, he couldn't remember what that had been. The cord snagged on the ceiling hook when he first threaded it through, but with time and patience, he achieved the desired length. He brought a chair from the kitchen to position under the loop.

Aidriel then set his affairs in order. Making sure his house was tidy, he collected all his important paperwork into a pile on the kitchen counter, laying what little money he had with it. The only items he could find to record his last words were an index card on which someone had scribbled a recipe for him, and a Sharpie, both in the bottom of his kitchen drawer. It didn't take him long to compose a brief message, and after spending several minutes searching his apartment for the best place to leave the note, he decided on taping it to the back of his hand. Then no one could possibly doubt his intentions.

Finally, Aidriel called Spiro, his neighbor down the hall who worked full-time, and left a message on his machine, asking that an ambulance be called. It might be days before someone discovered his body otherwise and there was no need to traumatize anyone.

Taking a deep breath, Aidriel stepped up onto the chair and placed the rope around his neck. He waited for a miraculous intervention; for Rubin to swoop in and stop him. He had not been harmed in over a week, so he knew an attack was due. The wind continued to blow noisily against the building, but there was no visitation. No voice calling for him to spare himself for one more day.

Aidriel steeled himself. He knew the hard part would be getting himself to start moving. Once the chair tipped over, the rope would take it from there.

"I'm free," he whispered, "in three…two…one…"

The chair toppled backward quickly and quietly, and the fall was short, but gentle. The noose slid up his neck, embracing the base of his skull, burning his skin.

Closing his eyes, Aidriel tried not to fight, not to breathe, not to acknowledge how truly afraid he was and how painful this death was. Jolts of involuntary movement pulsated through his limbs. His mind was surprisingly calm, guiding him through a leisurely tour of his senses as they failed one by one.

Goodbye vision. Goodbye feeling. Goodbye sound. Goodbye world.

Spiro was exactly five months younger than Aidriel, and sky blue eyed. There was a tattoo on his upper arm of a sparrow wearing a gas mask. He said it was meant to symbolize his readiness for whatever life could throw at him, which annoyed Aidriel, who found that worldview naïve.

"You can't possibly be ready for *any*thing that could come your way," Aidriel reasoned.

"Yes you can," Spiro insisted. "Every person can know themselves well enough to know how they will react to anything. They can decide how far they would go to save their own lives or someone else's, what they will refuse to be afraid of, where the boundaries of their moral structure lie, and how to keep their cool. That's all they need to be ready for any situation."

It was no accident that Spiro, slumped at his desk in customer service and feeling under the weather, was encouraged by his Passer to call it a day that overcast morning.

"Just go home," the ghost insisted. "It's better to just go home."

"It isn't a matter of life or death," Spiro mumbled miserably, messaging the ache behind his eyes.

"Perhaps it is."

Spiro was skeptical, but eventually gave in and clocked out, driving home wearing a grimace of pain. The blinds were still closed, so his apartment was wonderfully dark when he stepped inside. The light on his answering machine flashed like a small green winking eye amid the gloom, and holding his head, Spiro shuffled over to it.

"It's Aidriel from next door," the muffled voice on the old machine said.

"Hey," Spiro responded as if his neighbor was in the room with him. He took off his jacket with a smirk and placed it on the hook by the door. The smile vanished when he heard the rest of the message:

"When you get home, please call 911 for me. Thanks."

Aidriel had paused to let his words sink in, or to gather his thoughts, then he bid Spiro goodbye. His tone was serious and final.

Spiro turned so swiftly, he stepped through the icy fog of his Passer on his way to the hall. He dashed down the narrow, silent corridor, and pounded on Aidriel's door. There was no answer; the knob was not locked.

The image of the dangling body in the noose barely had a chance to register in Spiro's mind before he was out in the hall again, dashing back to his own home in a frenzy. He slammed through the door and knocked a lamp off his coffee table on his way to his closet. He had a bucket of tools there, on loan from his brother, hidden behind his heavy coat. Spiro had not seen his sibling since moving to this residence from his last duplex, where he had needed the tools. Every time he glimpsed them of late, he'd thought of what little use they were to him. However, in this moment of adrenaline-heightened panic, Spiro knew instantly what to do. He snatched the heavy-duty branch cutters and sprinted back to the neighboring apartment.

Aidriel's face was as gray as a Passer's by then. He swayed like a wet blanket on a clothesline when Spiro slammed into him. Fumbling at first, Spiro managed to position the rope inside the sharp beak of the cutters. With a squeeze, he severed the noose. Aidriel hit the couch with the side of his head as he fell, rolling into Spiro's legs, landing facedown.

Spiro was a very organized young man. It was not with detachment that he handled the situation at hand, but he did slip into his most productive mode, in which he ran through a swift checklist in his head as he moved.

Drop these. He tossed aside the clippers.

Call 911. Like most people his age, Spiro carried his mobile phone on his person, and handled it with the ease of familiarity as he dialed for help, turned on speakerphone, and laid it on the floor.

Get him breathing. This was the most difficult task on Spiro's list, but he moved without hesitation to roll Aidriel over. A check for a pulse was pointless, but he conducted it anyhow, loosening the noose and sliding it over the lifeless head.

219

Spiro was also a skilled multitasker and was not aware he had begun chest compressions while he answered the voice on his phone that asked him about his emergency. He calmly recited his address and told the other person that a man on the third floor had hanged himself.

"I'm doing CPR," he panted.

Aidriel looked serene, as if he were simply in a deep sleep. Spiro was not tired yet; his headache was forgotten. Behind him, his Passer appeared to be sitting bent forward on the overturned kitchen chair, its ghostly hands folded in its lap. Its opaque eyes watched with depraved fascination, a slight smile almost turning its lips.

"Is the man breathing?" asked the voice on the phone.

Without pausing in his brisk task, Spiro confidently and clearly answered, "Not yet."

CHAPTER 14

The town of Wellsburg, Iowa, would under normal circumstances be only a fifty-minute to an hour drive from Waterloo, but with the streets congested with Passers and pedestrians, it took longer. Progress was maddeningly slow, and everyone in the rented car remained for the most part silent.

Dreamer wanted to take Aidriel's hand again to reassure him, but he kept his tight grip on the door. St. Cross was remarkably calm, reading and making notes in his file.

They passed the sign welcoming them to Wellsburg at a snail's pace, and Todd made a stressed comment about every gawker in Iowa coming to see what was happening. There were police officers corralling walkers and directing traffic, turning away anyone coming to watch or just passing through.

Todd rolled down the window and told the police that they were going to the AGWSR Middle School, which was only partially true.

"That's where the action is," commented the officer distrustfully.

"Chester Williams sent for us," St. Cross lied, leaning over to see out the driver's side window and offering his I.D. The cop hesitated before taking it, stepping away to talk into his radio, his eyes on the card in his hand. Once the answer came, he asked for the names of the other three. It felt like an eternity that he spoke into his walkie and received answers back. Aidriel nervously tilted away from the window, watching the spirits drifting by.

When the policeman finally allowed them to pass and moved on to the next vehicle, St. Cross told Todd to find somewhere secluded to pull over, as close to the dead zone as possible.

"I think it best that you and I get out and try to find Williams to see if there's any way we can get Aidriel into the zone with little trouble."

"Yeah, I'm doubting that," said Todd, but he did as he was asked and pulled into the parking lot behind the middle school.

Unloading the folded-up wheelchair from the trunk, Todd helped St. Cross into it. The shrink made sure he had the plastic case that he had brought from the nightstand at home resting on his lap with the file, Aidriel's file. Taking a deep breath, Todd grasped the handles of the chair and pushed it into the crowd of Passers.

Waiting tensely, Dreamer glanced over at Aidriel and saw how composed he was. He watched the ghosts with a detached neutrality that comforted her a little. If he wasn't worried, why should she be?

"Do you think Williams can help?" she asked.

"Nope."

"What do you think will happen?"

Aidriel's hand moved down to grip the latch on the door, gazing steadily out through the

222

window in the direction St. Cross and Todd had gone.

"Where exactly is this dead zone?" he asked in lieu of responding.

"It's an intersection," Dreamer said. "Straight ahead, where West Jackson and West Fifth meet."

Aidriel continued to watch and wait, his keen gray eyes darting from face to face, his adrenaline rising. If he wasn't mistaken, the intersection she was talking about was at least six hundred feet away. Behind the parking lot was a vast field that ended in a baseball diamond at the intersection. The whole of the field and diamond was swarming with milling Passers, all of them facing the dead zone, waiting as if in a trance. Waiting for him.

"You okay?" asked Dreamer

"No…" Aidriel appeared to be realizing it as he said it. The familiar signals were there to warn him. The Passers walking by the car were beginning to slow. Some of them were turning their heads, looking at him, though they showed no sign of rage yet.

"I have to get out *now*," Aidriel said urgently. "Before the attack begins."

He swiftly unstrapped his seatbelt and threw open the door, Dreamer doing the same on her side. They couldn't spare the precious millisecond it would take to close the hatches again, and began to run instantly, following the direction of the street.

Dreamer had a little difficulty keeping up with Aidriel, but with effort, she caught his hand, falling into step beside him. They burst through the chilling clouds of spirits in their bid to reach the intersection, their shoes pounding the pavement.

There was a stiff wind blowing against them, making it hard to hear or breathe.

As he passed through them, Aidriel awakened the raw emotions that had driven the Passers to come here in the first place. They became animated, their faces contorting, their fingers becoming long, deadly claws. Shouts of wordless hatred went up, spreading through the midst of them in a wave. Once they were aware of him, they began to attack.

It all happened in a blur, but vividly and painfully. Aidriel's senses told him he was wading through a writhing mass of thorns, pulling Dreamer along beside him when she began to slow. She didn't appear to be harmed by the Passers themselves, but the fear and suffocating danger was driving her to panic. Her hand released his, and she fell behind; he was forced to run on without her. Of the two of them, she would be alright.

Ahead, Aidriel thought he could see where the wall of Passers ended and where the safe zone began. He had to keep his head down and his eyes mostly closed in defense against the flying ghost nails. They were digging into him and passing through him, snatching the air right out of his lungs. Everything burned and bled and he couldn't breathe or think, only run. A hundred, a thousand voices rose against him, drowning out calls from Dreamer or others to guide him. His cut, aching arms reached out ahead to force his path, to block his face, but there was no way to defend himself besides keeping on the move.

Aidriel tried to jump forward to gain ground but instead lost momentum, falling into the waiting grip of the Passers. He struggled until he could touch the street again and ran on, his head pounding with the blows that were caused by dashing through the spirits. The end was just ahead; he could see it, almost touch it. He reached out for it, and saw a glimpse of Rubin in the nearest circle, waiting for him. His Passer groped at the right moment, catching Aidriel's head in its long-fingered hands. It could have stopped his flight entirely if Dreamer had not been just steps behind him, slamming into him with enough force to drive him loose.

Falling into the dead zone, Aidriel and Dreamer regained their balance and continued to run, adrenaline coursing through their throbbing veins like electricity. Someone was loudly yelling words among the meaningless shrieks of the Passers, telling them to stop. Aidriel couldn't stop; there was too much fear and urgency to stop. He pressed onward, his speed increasing now that the Passers had fallen behind. There was still several feet of open space ahead; a wide circle of visible street.

Dreamer was dropping back, shouting for him to slow down. His body wouldn't listen; his mind was no longer commanding his actions. He continued to run full bore until a sound louder than the raised voices forcibly stopped him. His leg was yanked out from under him, and Aidriel fell flat on the pavement, skidding and half rolling, streaking blood, the reverberation of the gunshot echoing in his already ringing ears.

The Passers quieted to disappointed murmurings as Dreamer fell down beside him. Aidriel was in shock, and couldn't feel his leg. He looked down and saw a small crimson wound in his shin. He was bleeding everywhere.

Dreamer was a picture of terror, looking up and forward, slightly to their right; he followed her gaze. St. Cross was sitting just inside the dead zone, his plastic case open on his lap, a smoking pistol still in his hand.

"We told you to stop!" he called out. "The Passers were tricking you; the dead zone doesn't extend as far as they make it look, and if you'd gone too far, you would have run right out the other side."

"Drop the weapon!" shouted a police officer, drawing his own on St. Cross. Leaning precariously forward, the psychiatrist gently laid said gun on the pavement, raising his hands in surrender.

Aidriel rolled to his back in shock. His vision was blurring and he was shivering. It wasn't until now that he realized he and Dreamer were not alone inside the dead zone. There had to be at least half a dozen journalists with cameramen surveying the area, not to mention the police, St. Cross, deTarlo, Williams and his assistant, and Todd.

"You're a lousy damn shot!" Chester Williams yelled in anger, aggressively approaching St. Cross as several cops did. "Lotta good you did, blowing a hole in him!"

"Sir, stay back!" one of the officers ordered, physically forcing Williams to do so. St. Cross put his hands on the back of his head and the lawmen roughly felt him for other weapons. He spoke too quietly for Aidriel or Dreamer to hear, but the cops became calmer and allowed him to lower his arms.

One of the other officers lifted his radio to his mouth and began to call for an ambulance, but deTarlo caught him by the wrist and shook her head.

Aidriel felt he must be falling into delirium, because nothing was making sense. Why weren't the cops arresting St. Cross for shooting him? Why was deTarlo telling them not to summon help?

"The Passers said not to interfere," she reminded the officer.

Dreamer bunched up her jacket and put it under Aidriel's head, moving out of his range of hazy vision briefly. He felt his leg move and figured she must be attempting to stop the blood loss. She was talking to him in a strained voice, trying to sound brave. It crossed his mind to say something to reassure her, but he didn't see the point. She was not the one bleeding in the middle of the street.

"It's fine," he mumbled thickly. "This has happened before."

Dreamer was no expert, but she was pretty sure he was going into shock. The shot was a clear-through that had probably hit one of the nearby houses, but she couldn't get the hemorrhaging to stop on both sides. It was pooling around her knees. She looked around desperately. Everyone was just standing there, watching!

"Why won't someone help him?" she cried out, feeling herself come unglued.

"I'm calling for an ambulance, lady," the police officer with the radio told deTarlo definitively. She shrugged and shifted her balance from one heel to the other.

"It'll take too long to get here now, with the traffic," she said. "Besides, he has a DNR."

"What?" asked St. Cross, shocked.

"He signed it days ago," deTarlo said nonchalantly. "It's on his tag if you don't believe me. Said he wanted some control over when the study would end."

"Why did you let him do that?" demanded Chester. DeTarlo raised her eyebrows as if it were outside of her control, adjusting her glasses on the bridge of her nose.

"Somebody get me something to use as a tourniquet!" Dreamer called out, gripping Aidriel's leg with both hands. She looked around to see if any of the people watching helplessly from a distance were going to move. They were all staring, enthralled, but keeping their distance; even the police officers. What in the world was wrong with them?

Aidriel laid still and listened to the goings-on around him. His hands were getting tingly, and the spottiness of his vision was worsening. He felt as if he were falling asleep, and could think only that he didn't want that. Sitting up swiftly caused temporary dizziness, but Aidriel could see well enough to realize Rubin was inside the dead zone.

Dreamer saw his eyes focus and he became still. Glancing over her shoulder, she looked swiftly back to Aidriel, the fear apparent on her face.

"How did he…?" she whispered. "He broke the rule."

It was not the first time Rubin had done so, neither was it the first time Dreamer saw a Passer that did. There was an unwritten rule among the spirits, it seemed, that they could not get directly involved in the world. They often threw things, slammed doors, shook beds, made the floors groan, supplied their companions with information all the time, but they were not supposed to attack with their hands as they had been doing, and they were never allowed to directly change something.

When Dreamer was ten, she and her Girl Scout troop went into the woods at a national park on a camping trip. A few of them had wandered off in search of firewood and to explore, and she'd intentionally lost sight of all others. She'd liked the solitude, and felt that perhaps she was visiting the borderlands of heaven until the bear appeared.

But Tracy was there. The Passer had always been young-looking and cynical. It tried to steer Dreamer's decision-making, but the girl was too frightened to follow directions. So Tracy broke the rule and took a heavy stick to the bear's face, startling it and driving it away. It might have saved Dreamer's life, and though the incident left a lasting impression, she had never thought too much about what her Passer had actually done. But now as Tracy stepped through the invisible barrier to stand beside Rubin, Dreamer realized the long-term ramifications of breaking the rules.

Aidriel began to have difficulty maintaining focus. His awareness of his situation was fading, his anxiety with it. His blood was still seeping around Dreamer's fingers with no sign of stopping. It was hot and thin; the aspirin he had been taking nearly constantly for the last several days was probably contributing to his continuous hemorrhaging. He lay back down on the street, his head on her jacket, and relaxed, breathing easier.

"Hang in there," Dreamer encouraged. There was that phrase again, and that word: *hang*. And here he was once more on the threshold of death.

Neither of them noticed the silent approach of the Passers. Before Dreamer could react, Rubin flung her aside with enough force to dislodge her grip on Aidriel's leg. She wiped the blood from her hands on her jeans and stood up, turning and watching briefly in shock. Tracy put its hands around Aidriel's throat and placed its feet on either side of him, holding him up and strangling him. He tried to grip the ghost's arms, tried to pull free, but he was too tired. Rubin put one hand under Aidriel's head, and placed the other over his nose and mouth.

"Let it go, my friend," the Passer said almost soothingly. "Release it and the pain will fade away."

"Tracy, please!" Dreamer pleaded, her eyes glassy. She was horrified and grieved to watch a Passer she had known and trusted for years turn against her. Tracy acted as if it didn't hear Dreamer.

Aidriel's body went into convulsions as he was asphyxiated. His head fell back, despite Rubin's hand, and in his vision, the smoky forms of the watching crowd of ghosts faded into a featureless pale cloud that emitted a lightless haze. He felt as if his very spirit were rising up out of him, gathering into a tight wad in his windpipe. The arch in his back became more exaggerated; his arms bent in close to his body, his hands involuntarily gripping at nothing on either side of his chest. All the life and energy in him was gathering in his windpipe, at the base of his neck, and the force of the spirit's struggle to escape was pulling him up so the rest of him hung limply around his levitating throat.

If he had been able to see anything past the gathering of Passers, he would have realized the horizon was literally upside down, as it appeared in the hallucinations during his earlier deaths. His leg continued to bleed, draining him of all heat, so he began to tremble with cold.

"Release it," Rubin urged him, "and the pain will fade away."

Tracy tightened its grip so Aidriel could not take in another breath. They were surprised, however, when Dreamer swiped a blood-streaked hand through her Passer.

"Let go of him!" the phlebotomist demanded.

Instantly, to the shock of everyone watching, Tracy obeyed and inched away from Aidriel. Rubin continued to support Aidriel's upper back, its free hand hovering over him, prepared to snatch away his spirit when it broke free. Dreamer was moments away from demanding that Rubin stand down also, but she never got the chance. Tracy launched at her, choking her into silence.

The stunned watchers around the dead zone gasped but could not interfere as Tracy strangled the breath right out of Dreamer without a hint of hesitation or remorse. Aidriel was too dead himself to know what was happening, but Dreamer kept her eyes on him through her tears. Even as she collapsed and suffocated, she saw the hazy form expanding from Aidriel's throat and into Rubin's grasp.

Aidriel could not resist death any longer; as his spirit rose and escaped, Rubin released his body and let it fall back to the street. The mist took on a visibly human form, and Aidriel the Passer looked around him, his face a picture of loss.

"Finally," he murmured, as if admitting to something he knew would eventually come. Tracy became distracted to see him, and released

231

Dreamer, so she also dropped lifelessly to the pavement. Though hasty, the strangulation had been effective, and Dreamer's Passer found it easier to exit her mortal shell than Aidriel had been able to. She threw herself upon his ghost, gripping him around the chest, but Tracy and Rubin were already starting to drag Aidriel into them, devouring and absorbing him.

"No, don't let them!" Dreamer screamed. "*Now* you can't let them have control!"

The last word echoed through Aidriel's thoughts like a bell's peal, and suddenly it all made sense. From the very start, it had all been about the control. He had never taken charge of anything after he was first attacked, and over time, he had less and less control over his life. During the last several weeks in particular, he had had no say whatsoever in what was happening to him, and that was exactly how the Passers wanted it in leading up to this moment. Control was what they had stolen away from him at all cost, and was of the greatest import now, even outside of his body.

Aidriel looked to the sky, and there was a flash of lightning in his psyche, illuminating his vision from the corners inward, so he could no longer see the natural world. The change inside him was instantaneous. He could resolutely determine his path, and could witness it open before him like a complex passageway, the surface of which told the future and the past in intersecting designs that he created at will with unrealized skill. In his revelation he saw the faces and immediately knew the names and stories of every one of the by-now thousands of Passers encircling the intersection. If he desired, his range of view and knowledge of the

232

ghosts could extend across the whole surface of the Earth. Their combined being was vast and complex in his mind's eye; a conscious glittering cloud of spectral nebulae, the smallest detail of which was a world within a world and could reveal everything. He could sense how many of them were rule breakers on a lesser level; hangers-on to existence in the world when they had fulfilled their purpose and should pass on to the next.

The ghosts knew the spiritual world would change, and every Passer on the planet had wanted to see the spectacle, even if there was no role for them to play in bringing about the result. The fate of their passive invasion hung in the balance but their presence at the dead zone was no last-ditch effort. It had never been their intention to beat Aidriel to death; they'd come to see his awakening and share, if only briefly while he connected with them, in his all-encompassing power. Dreamer had been right in her assumption that the existence of the Passers was an upset to the balance; an accidental tipping of the scales that the spirits had chosen to exploit for their own insatiable thirst for control. But the Passers had mistakenly thought that the weblike union of power that Aidriel would initiate could be shared. He was not their equal; the rules they broke did not apply to him.

Shedding the defenselessness like an unwanted cloak, Aidriel felt the world opening up to him. His sense of being smothered evaporated. He slipped out of the grasp of Rubin, Tracy, even Dreamer, and stood upright and vibrant as if he were still in mortal form. With just a turn of his ghostly head, an electromagnetic disturbance poured out from him like an earthquake of sound, and he commanded complete control of every Passer, everywhere. The ghosts' underlying current of hatred and greed for power vanished. On every continent, the Passers stopped in their tracks, their instinct to come find him vanishing. They blinked and turned and went back to where they had been. The shifting clouds of smoky spirits thinned before the eyes of those that saw them as many of the Passers vanished from existence. For too long the "guidance" of the ghosts had overwhelmed the wills of their charges and with the control of the dead in his hands, Aidriel could restore the balance again in favor of the living.

A simultaneous sigh arose from the Passers in Wellsburg that was nearly deafening. They raised their voices in a wordless plea for mercy—to have their hopes at greater power fulfilled, but Aidriel could see through them and into their intentions; he cast them out and across the divide into eternity. The journalists, cameramen and police wheeled about in surprise, their eyes and lenses surveying the mob as it began to vanish; Aidriel spared nearly none of them in his undoing of their Sentience coup. Soon all that remained of the nonliving were Rubin and Tracy within the dead zone, and Rod, Kara and Andrei on the outside.

Rod turned to Chester, its mood immensely sad.

"Can you understand what this means?" it asked. Williams was watching with a stare a bit less awestruck and confused than the others, and he nodded faintly.

"There's a hierarchy among the Passers," he whispered. It meant that the Passers had seen the future, and did not want to be controlled. There was an order of their actions that had been laid out, and they knew they had to fulfill it. If driving Aidriel to madness would strip from him the truth of his power when he died, and attacking him until he had no control was the only way to do so, they would do it. All the others they had tormented had forfeited their rights to mastership when they killed themselves; even their spirits did not realize the truth of what they had given up, and if they did, they chose to do nothing about it. But Aidriel had not taken kindly to the Passers' methods for mass rule and had punished them.

St. Cross looked up as if startled out of a trance when Chester spoke, and became animated with his hands.

"I was right!" he exclaimed. "There is truth in the hidden meaning of the Paradox!"

"Meaning what?" asked deTarlo. She was scribbling as fast as she could on her clipboard, teetering dangerously on her heels as if she might fall over. Her quick eyes gauged the agitated law officers around, and she cocked her ear to catch the sound of an ambulance siren in the distance.

"Meaning Aidriel was tried by fire to take his place as..." St. Cross's voice trailed off when a bloodcurdling howl rose in Rubin's mouth.

Sometimes the Passers resisted when it was time to pass on into the afterlife, the next step of their three-plane journey. They were usually harmless while it was happening, but it was frightening to see and hear this take place all the same. With Aidriel's change and the submission of the ghosts, the time of the afflicters had abruptly ended. Tracy hid its face in grief at the realization, but rose and faded without a struggle at Aidriel's silent command. Rubin, however, was a breaker of rules; it could still save the remaining Passers from their newly crowned master's control if it removed the master. It seized Aidriel and tried to drag him up into the air as it evaporated.

"Don't let it happen!" cried out Kara, starting forward. There were only moments to prevent it, and had Dreamer not been a Passer also, she would have been forced to watch helplessly. But there was a reason that Tracy had strangled her to death, even if the Passer had acted merely in hatred. She leapt and embraced Aidriel from behind, ordering with strong authority, "Rubin, pass on alone!"

This moment was the reason St. Cross had felt Dreamer needed to meet Aidriel. It was not only that Tracy broke the rules when it attacked the bear; it broke the rules to obey Dreamer's order to do so. There was something about the girl's words that demanded obedience from the spirits. Somehow, the shrink seemed to know she was the one to help Aidriel save himself.

In the twinkling of an eye, Rubin was gone, though Aidriel continued to drift upward. Dreamer did not have to struggle to pull him back to earth. Falling down as if to her knees, she guided him onto his back over his body, ensuring he returned to it. Though his mortal shell was damaged, the bleeding in his leg had stopped when his heart did.

No pain of leaving his body or nearly doing so the many times before compared to the white-hot agony that bathed him to return to life. He sucked in a breath and convulsed as he had in death, the still-healing injury on the back of his head scraping across the pavement, his arms and hands again squeezing in close to his chest. Dropping limp, he turned and saw Dreamer lying beside him.

Her brown hair spread out beneath her head like a carpet, her limbs lying gracefully as if she was sleeping; but her skin was gray, her lips blue. Her Passer lay down upon her body, superimposing a cloudy reflection over the lifeless form. But the ghost began to weep.

"I can't return to it," she murmured.

All the pain of his injuries swept over Aidriel like they always did when he was revived, yet with effort he rolled to his side. He lifted his aching head, and dragged his arm up to reach for her.

"Yes, you can," he said hoarsely.

They were stronger when their hands met; that must be why they so often had an unexplainable urge to hold hands.

Dreamer's Passer closed her eyes and sighed slowly, vanishing into her body. She experienced the same burning unpleasantness to be reborn, reeling and gasping, her senses too shell-shocked to take in anything at first. Someone held her hand, and when she opened her eyes, she could see. It was Aidriel.

CHAPTER 15

The most important thing on deTarlo's mind as she craned her neck to see into the ambulance was publishing her study. Aidriel was semiconscious and looked like a dead body under the hurrying hands of the paramedics. They were hastily bandaging his leg so he'd make it to the hospital and were preparing a transfusion.

Dreamer was sitting on a stretcher several feet away, a blanket around her trembling shoulders, her hands holding an air mask to her face and sucking in the wonderful oxygen. She was trying to croak something to the EMT examining her bruised throat, but he kept shushing her.

"He's AB positive," she insisted. "Listen to me; I was there for some of his care."

The paramedic took it under advisement and called it to his fellows.

DeTarlo stepped away from the ambulance and strode over to the phlebotomist as yet a another police vehicle arrived. The psychologist had her precious clipboard tucked in her arm against her side, and was swinging Aidriel's dog tag deliberately with the other. When she and the additional people present had converged on Aidriel and Dreamer, she was sure that above all else, she got a hold of his tag. He'd made it through the hard part. She would hate for him to die now because of his DNR order when she desperately needed him to finish her report. She could already visualize the study being published, and the thrill gave her goose bumps.

"Are you alright?" the shrink asked Dreamer, her eyes on the activity around them. The phleb just nodded, keeping the mask over her face. The EMT had left her briefly, and she gingerly felt the nasty bruising on her neck. She glanced toward the open ambulance, but couldn't see Aidriel.

"He okay?" she asked huskily, motioning.

"He'll survive." DeTarlo smiled broadly and authentically. Dreamer mirrored her and pointed at the dog tag.

"Thank you," she whispered. "For taking that."

DeTarlo smirked again, claiming it was her pleasure, then wandering off to find Williams while the paramedic returned to load Dreamer into the ambulance.

Chester stood facing the empty baseball diamond, talking rapidly on his Bluetooth and poking around on his touchpad. He paused in his chatter to send his assistant off with a wave of his hand to talk to some local officials. St. Cross and Todd were speaking to the police who stood guard around the psychiatrist, though what about, she had no idea. The cops had witnessed everything they had. All of them continuously waved off the questions and pleas of the journalists, especially Williams, who was becoming agitated. The police photographer had finished taking pictures of the scene long after the media had, and someone was hosing the blood off the street. There was not a single Passer in sight.

Giving up on any interviews, most of the reporters and their crews dashed off to their vehicles, many of them talking on their cells, desperate to be the first to break the story. DeTarlo loved the circus; she was the ringmaster. No one could get to Aidriel except through her, and at the moment, she would not let anyone close to him. She had all the answers to the questions the law and media asked, and she said not a word more than she wanted.

The ambulance slammed its doors, its siren wailing as it sped off in the direction of the hospital in Waterloo. Williams finished a call and paused before making another.

"Chester, Ana." St. Cross got their attention and motioned them over to talk. The police took several reluctant paces away, but watched the psychiatrist closely, assuming correctly he couldn't go far. Williams and deTarlo took places as near to him as they could to keep the conversation private, ignoring Todd, who hovered nearby.

"Let's get something out in the open, shall we?" began St. Cross. "Aidriel is my patient, has been from the beginning, and I can guarantee that I can overturn any paperwork you might have that says otherwise."

DeTarlo opened her mouth to respond but he motioned for her to listen.

"That being said," he continued, smacking his lips at the beginning of his sentences, "any and *all* decisions about his participation, opinion, and well-being from here on out are *his*, and none of us can say otherwise. He was released from the psych ward under your recommendations, Ana, and as far as I know, has complete control over his own welfare. But I don't necessarily get first dibs on him, and our…plans…don't have to be contradictory."

"My study has a conclusion very different than what I hypothesized," said deTarlo. "And though I am not usually pleased to admit being wrong, the patient has proved to be a very interesting subject, and will continue to be so, I'm sure."

"Do you have any idea what he means for the Sentience Movement?" asked Chester with excited animation. "Everything we thought we knew about Passers could change! With his help, I can revolutionize the world of Passerists!"

"What makes any of you think he'll do what you want?" asked Todd, forgetting his place. "Dreamer said they ditched you guys because you're so dang bossy."

Williams rolled his eyes and deTarlo just smiled patiently.

"I could prolong my study for years," said Ana.

"Kelly Road was not officially closed," added Chester. "Akimos still has obligations to fulfill."

"Why does this have to end in exploitation?" asked St. Cross bitterly, feeling the utter helplessness that his physical condition imposed upon him.

"Everyone saw your little sharpshooter stunt," Williams pointed out. "It's lucky for you that the cops are just taking you in for procedure and are buying the lie that you were aiming at the Passers and missed. We could have you shut out entirely."

"This isn't about me!" St. Cross exclaimed. "Aidriel has been to hell and back, and now you

242

want to interrogate and study him for another lifetime."

Ana and Chester didn't argue, neither did they appear remorseful.

"This isn't about *us*," said Williams. "Can you imagine the power he has? We know he can control the Passers while in the same form as they, but perhaps he can do it while alive also! Who knows what he could accomplish in cooperation with *A.S.M.*? The possibilities are endless and awesome!"

"We're very fortunate to already have a foot in the door," agreed deTarlo. "The patient can make our lives very profitable. Our writings will be taken as reliable information for generations to come, at least."

"Aidriel's not going to go along with that," St. Cross insisted. "I've known him longer than both of you have, and I *know* that I understand him better. He's endured the rarity of his situation for years, and this could mean an *end* to it. Can you imagine living every day with such fear? He's thought of nothing but Passers for the last twelve years; if he has an opportunity to leave it all behind now, he will."

Williams didn't appear moved, and deTarlo simply shrugged.

"He'll have to put his retirement on hold," she said dismissively. "He still has legally binding obligations."

St. Cross knew she was right and could not think of anything he could do. He didn't bother to argue further, and slumped back in his chair, his green eyes fixed sadly on Ana's face. She adjusted her tortoiseshell spectacles and looked at her clipboard, ignoring him. Chester turned away to tap his ear device and listened a moment before saying they'd be there soon.

"Aidriel and Dreamer have no next of kin available," he told deTarlo. "They want me to sign them in at the hospital."

He looked around for his assistant, but the slight man was still busy in conversation with the officials and clearly could not be torn away. Leaving him to find his own way was the decision Chester made with a shrug. Without a word, deTarlo lowered her clipboard and fell into step beside Williams as they headed off toward his car.

St. Cross grimly watched them go, his mind racing for ways to prevent them. It would be a lengthy battle, he knew, but there was no convincing them. His best course of action was to post bail, get back to Fort Wayne and start looking for the loophole to get Aidriel out of any commitments.

"There's the car," Todd said, jogging over to a police car that had pulled up by the curb. The nurse oversaw a pair of officers that opened the trunk and began moving things to make room for the psychiatrist's wheelchair. St. Cross sat in thought for several more minutes before he sensed Andrei standing beside him. After having seen how uncommon rule breakers were among the spirits, he became fascinated with the idea.

"Why did you break the rules?" the shrink asked the Passer. "Why'd you push the ladder?"

Andrei looked down at him grimly. Its gaze passed over the people still moving about around them.

"Because," Andrei said finally, "if you had not fallen, you would be on the road to Waterloo already, and you would not be sitting here waiting, where it's safe."

"Safe?"

Andrei didn't elaborate and replied, "You will be well looked after. Goodbye, my friend." Breaking into a run, the ghost dashed up the street in the direction the vehicles were leaving from, vanishing from sight.

The ambulance was roomy; there was enough space for Dreamer to sit quietly to the side, clutching the oxygen mask to her face, while Aidriel lay serenely on the stretcher. His skin was so ashen he still appeared dead, but the paramedics seemed for the moment unconcerned, or preoccupied.

Taking several deep breaths, Dreamer pulled the mask from her face to speak.

"I'm outside it now," she whispered hoarsely.

Aidriel turned his head to look up at her, his eyes too dull to convey his wordless question.

"The... network," Dreamer explained with a small wave of her hand at an invisible strand of spider silk, as before. "I'm outside of it now, like you. We're tuned in to one another now, aren't we?"

With heavy eyelids, Aidriel blinked slowly and nodded. He painfully raised one arm to motion at his own shoulder with his hand that the weight had been lifted. Dreamer leaned forward to grasp his fingers, kissing them and letting go. He managed a smile.

Mirroring him, Dreamer put her mask over her face and sat back, relaxing.

Rod and Kara stood on either side of Chester's car when Williams and deTarlo got into the front seats.

"Where are you going?" Rod asked, leaning over to see in the window.

"The hospital."

"Don't do what you plan to do," Kara tried to convince them. "We can observe the outcome, and no good shall come of it for you."

DeTarlo laughed slightly.

"As far as we know," she said, "neither of you can be heeded until further notice."

Williams looked at her, surprised.

"I don't agree with that," he stated. "Rod has been nothing but trustworthy."

"Only when the patient isn't around."

"Well, he's *not* around."

"Not at the moment. That's why neither of you," she now spoke to the Passers, "are coming with us. Kara, go back to Fort Wayne."

"Did you not witness the event?" asked Kara softly.

"*Go*," ordered Ana.

"Kara," Rod said, its face telling the other spirit that it didn't have to obey.

Without responding, Kara turned and took a step away, concealing itself from the psychologist, though Williams could watch it leaving.

"Chester," Rod began again. "Heed our warning. I can see *how* you will be of continuing help to him."

"Chet," deTarlo said, steely. "Start the car. We need to get to the hospital before the reporters do."

Williams resisted, his hand resting on the keys in the ignition, but not turning them.

"*Chet*," deTarlo repeated, harshly. "Unless you'd prefer to go back to Denver to deal with the fire and protests, *start the car*."

He looked at her, unyielding. He *did* want to return to Denver. That wasn't the issue.

"Kelly Road is mine only," he demanded. "You don't set another foot in that building unless I say so."

Dr. deTarlo's eyes burned angrily, but she forced a smile.

"We'll discuss this later."

"No, I'm not your errand boy. You can conduct your own studies when and wherever you want. But the Bird Cage is off limits."

"Alright," Ana said like a long-suffering parent. "We need to leave."

Williams started the car and shifted into drive, speeding off and leaving Rod standing alone in the street. The Passer watched them go sadly, then walked over to fall into step beside St. Cross as Todd was wheeling him to the police car.

"My friend," Rod said softly. "Prepare for the change."

Williams and deTarlo were still debating heatedly when they turned a corner at a stop sign, starting down a road with nothing but trees and a lake on either side. Ana was razzing Chester for choosing the longer route to Waterloo to avoid traffic. Besides a semitruck coming in the opposite

247

direction, the street ahead appeared empty. Distracted and anxious, Ana cast a prolonged glance at the road ahead. She did not see the delayed flash of realization on Chester's face as he stared out the windshield, his gifted eyes discerning the hazy outline of an invisible Passer.

Had he not been able to see the spirit, Chester would not have reacted the way he did. There was only a moment for the image before his eyes to register in his brain, and Williams's subconscious mind told him he was on a collision course with a person. His hands responded instinctively, jolting the wheel to avoid hitting the humanlike form, but he overcompensated. The car swerved wildly into the other lane, and deTarlo screamed.

They collided head-on with a solid tree and Ana went crashing forward through the windshield, the car spinning to the side after her. The back wheel of the vehicle struck a mound of soil just short of where the psychologist had landed. For the briefest of moments, a ringing silence descended in the midst of the clunking made by the damaged engine, then the semi blared its horn, riding the brakes. It was too close to stop.

Williams was shaken but unhurt, and was lifting his head from the steering wheel airbag when the truck hit the back of the car. The smaller vehicle swung around off the road, metal shrieking. Smashing into the short guardrail on the lake side, it flipped over it and rolled down the short ledge, landing upside down on the water with enough force to crack any windows that were still intact.

Chester found himself lying on his head at an angle, the water gushing in through the hole in the windshield and surrounding him. He could feel the car sinking at a terrifying rate and struggled to loosen his seatbelt. The latch was stuck. The airbag was crowding him, hogging precious space. Twisting and pulling, Chester began to panic. The water had risen around his head and was submerging his chest. It took a lot of effort to bend far enough to get his face above the surface to gasp for air.

The groaning of the car drowned out any sound outside. He heard the sloshing of the water rushing in, and the clinking of his rings against the windows as he thrashed about. There was no noise of help coming; no audible voices.

By the time Williams got the seatbelt loose and rolled over, the water had almost entirely filled the inside of the vehicle. The passenger airbag blocked any escape through the windshield. He struggled and kicked at the side windows, yelling out wordlessly or shouting Ana's name. Not that he thought she was still alive. It was instinct; his panicked psyche couldn't think of anyone else to call to.

The water was frigid and Chester was having difficulty breathing, pressing against the roof of the car in his last desperate seconds, using the buoyant airbag for support.

It suddenly came to his mind how Rod had told him that it witnessed the first time Aidriel had drowned. Chester realized that Rod could have saved him from drowning also, if only he had listened to it. Now no one was going to save him.

Letting exhaustion take over, Williams closed his eyes and permitted the water to pull him under, sliding beneath the airbag. He couldn't get enough momentum to kick out the windows. They were cracked—why wouldn't they break? All of his wealth and influence meant nothing now, when the only thing he needed was a hammer. He should have listened to Rod; he should have ignored deTarlo. Chester held his breath until it hurt; his breathing instinct took over and he had to exhale. Water rushed into his lungs, and the suffering increased. His air was gone.

Lying on the embankment above, Ana thought she was flat on her stomach, but couldn't feel anything to know. Her head was turned toward the road, and she'd heard the semi slam into Chester's car, then stutter on the blacktop as the driver deployed the brakes, skidding at an angle so his truck blocked both lanes.

The car had smashed into the water. She could hear Williams screaming her name, and when his voice stopped, she began to involuntarily weep. The semi driver was panicking on the road, and ran over to her, roughly shaking her back. She wanted to shriek for him to leave her alone; that Chester was drowning. But Ana had no control over her body and could only lie there in shock and cry.

Out of the corner of her eye, she saw the road embraced in a cloud of smoke. Andrei stood in the middle of the street, examining the result of its endeavor to indirectly destroy their car. Like Rubin and Tracy, it was not long of the world. But it had seen what would happen and how the Passers would fall back into place now that those two rebellious spirits were gone; it knew what it had to do, and it had done it.

Andrei waited until Williams stopped yelling and looked to Ana as the driver ran down the bank into the water to swim toward the submerged vehicle. Satisfied, the last of the rule-breaking Passers turned and walked several steps away before drifting upward and vanishing from the earth.

CHAPTER 16

Aidriel was suddenly awakened to his name being uttered; an icy hand rested on his shoulder. His eyes flew open and he looked up in the semidarkness. The Passer of Chester Williams stood over him, apprehensive and urgent.

"Get up," Chester said. "They're coming for you."

Instantly wide awake, Aidriel threw off his blanket, dropping his bare feet to the floor and standing. It had been more than a year since the bullet had torn through his leg, and though on days of inclement weather it pained him, Aidriel could still move without assistance.

When he had awakened in the hospital and learned about the accident that had left Chester dead and deTarlo paralyzed, he had felt an unexplainable remorse. There were some newspaper articles tacked to his wall about it, proclaiming the tragedy of the leading voice in Passerism's drowning. "PASSERIST CHESTER WILLIAMS KILLED IN TRAGIC AUTO CRASH: PSYCHOLOGIST CRITICISED FOR BLAMING PASSERS," one blared in bold black letters, while another read, "AMERICAN SENTIENCE MOVEMENT WITHOUT

WILLIAMS: HOW A.S.M. IS MOURNING AND MOVING FORWARD."

Williams's friend Fagin McPike had taken over leadership of the organization; he was charismatic but not as gifted as his predecessor. Chester's only contact with *A.S.M.* was to keep it at a distance from Aidriel. Williams was survived by a daughter and fiancée, and had not, as far as Aidriel knew, gone to see them since his death. It was depressing.

There were also articles expounding upon how deTarlo, having survived the crash, was being chastised for blaming the ghosts. The idea of Passers harming anyone was truly ridiculous now, because they never did. From the moment Aidriel had taken control of them, not one had broken the rule, except for Andrei in its efforts to ensure the Passer companion of Aidriel would be a worthy helper.

As a result, he had not felt the need to test his power of command over the spirits since he returned to his mortal body. Even being in his company so often, Chester had never suggested he try. Perhaps the Paradox of Natural Judgment no longer applied. But Aidriel should have fled like Williams had told him to the first time the ghost came to give him counsel. If he had, perhaps deTarlo wouldn't have found him when she recovered.

Chester moved to the door and motioned at the knob; there wasn't time for Aidriel to take anything. Silently slipping out into the hall, Aidriel glanced about for the nurses or orderlies, but he saw no one and heard nothing but distant classical music. It was well past midnight, and the psych ward was asleep.

With Williams a step behind him, Aidriel crept down the hallway until he stood outside the closed room with two cardboard name tags next to it. One said "Dreamer Akimos," his wife's name.

Being in such a contained environment as the psych ward had been surprisingly beneficial in the swift courtship and engagement of Aidriel and Dreamer. It had been nothing like she expected when she checked herself in to be near him and then could not get out again. She'd been so angry at first; he'd been resigned. She sulked in her room and wept sorely at Tracy's betrayal. There was little privacy; everyone heard the sweet nothings he whispered to her or soon heard of them through the gossip circuit. There were no cobwebs to clean or rugs to shake or milkshakes to make, but they made do the best they could when she was happy enough to. They read to each other or argued over facts they couldn't prove. He called her beautiful, and she called him perfect, and the other patients called the nurses on them when they tried to be alone.

Chester had watched from a distance as they bounced in and out of psychiatric institutions and the fourth floor of the hospital after attempts at escape caused them injury. Dreamer dreamt of freedom and cried with frustration and at the ups and downs caused by her medication and her long-lasting mourning at the loss of her Passer companion. Aidriel got his hands on a guitar and sang Jason Mraz's "I'm Yours" until she smiled again.

He'd asked her to marry him in the dead of night while her roommate snored a few feet away.

Williams's former assistant smuggled them rings and a small bouquet and the paperwork to make their secret ceremony official. The nurses and doctors Aidriel knew from the ER came to congratulate him and ensured Dreamer's ID bracelet was updated. Nothing had changed, but Aidriel began to spend hours at the windows, counting the steps in his mind from the front doors to a safe distance from the hospital. The shuttle could take them to the far end of the parking lot, then maybe they'd have a chance.

Aidriel opened the door to Dreamer's room and went in without a sound, leaving it open with Chester guarding it. Kara stood by the window dressed in its usual nightgown, gazing down into the street, and it turned to watch. Passers were no longer a foreign sight in hospitals, thanks to Aidriel's "electromagnetic pulse of change," as deTarlo referred to it. She liked to talk about him in his presence, as if he were deaf or not there. She'd opened up shop in the hospital and enjoyed the benefits of the popularity of her papers among the psychological field, throwing her commanding weight around whenever a more permanent solution for Aidriel and Dreamer was discussed among her peers. He had known for a while that the time would come when the overbearing woman who called herself his psychologist would have the "remarkable Akimoses" moved to the Bird Cage, which she had weaseled and wormed and fought for nearly a year to pry from the hands of *A.S.M.* It seemed the time had finally come.

Dreamer was lying on her side on the bed, dozing under a cloud of sedatives. She was less cooperative with their wardens than he was of late and often had to be restrained with prescription drugs. Aidriel did not attempt to wake her, but gathered her up in his arms, leaving the blanket.

Chester motioned that it was safe to proceed, but that they needed to hurry. Aidriel darted down the hall toward the double doors before the elevator with the nurse's station behind the windows. He slowed and realized he had no plan to continue, but spotted a Passer on the other side that he recognized. It was Matilda. The lock buzzed and he pushed quietly through, smiling in thanks at Tammy the nurse as he passed where she sat. She mouthed, "Take care" but didn't dare make a sound.

Aidriel elbowed the elevator button and it immediately opened. Stepping in, still cradling Dreamer and with Kara and Chester a pace behind, he faced forward once more. In his haste to get through, he had pushed one of the double doors open so far it had remained that way. He could see down the hall to the opposite end of the floor, and when the distant lock buzzed, he could observe the people arriving through the other double doors.

St. Cross was leading the way, dressed in a smartly pressed suit, Rod a step behind him. The police officers and orderlies held the door open for deTarlo to ride through in her motorized wheelchair. The poetic justice had not been lost on St. Cross when he had regained the use of his legs after Ana became confined to the chair, though it had had no affect on their roles of authority. One squeeze of the trigger had cost him his license, and it had only been through begging and flattery that he had managed to convince Dr. deTarlo to include him in her studies, if only so she could access his extensive experience with Aidriel.

Ana didn't look far enough down the hall to see the other elevator, but St. Cross did. He spotted the man cradling his wife, both of them dressed in white and barefoot. He was pretty sure Aidriel saw him too, but did not return the shrink's smile. The elevator hatch closed, and Tammy hurriedly pushed the swinging door shut, the lock humming.

DeTarlo drove past St. Cross, rudely clipping the back of his leg with her chair in her rush to get to Aidriel's room. He didn't bother to tell her it was a waste of time.

Chester must have warned Aidriel. They'd come for him, but he was gone.

42.432284, -92.934793

47459214R00143

Made in the USA
Charleston, SC
08 October 2015